MIRACLES AND MARRIAGE
Making a Family Series, Book Five

BARBARA MCMAHON

Chapter One

Zoe Blackstone sat bundled up in an old quilt. The wind blew from the sea, the tang of salt filling the air. It was too cold to be outside, but she snuggled in the warmth of the quilt and stared out at the gray sea. It had been raining until a half hour ago. The gray skies looked as if they melded into the water at the horizon. It was a dreary day. One that suited her mood to perfection. Tears welled again. Sniffing, she refused to cry.

Staring over the deserted beach from the family cottage, she tried to make her mind go blank—but the doctor's words echoed over and over. Her recommendation—a hysterectomy.

Zoe blinked back the tears. She was only twenty-eight, far too young to face this. Never married, she still held the hope she'd find the man of her dreams one day and get married and start a family. That wouldn't happen if she had the operation. She'd thought she had all the time in the world. Instead she was limited to months.

The painful menstrual cramps and heavy bleeding contributed to her being almost incapacitated several days each month. If she wanted relief from the pain, this was the option her physician recommended. She snuggled against the hot water bottle pressed to her abdomen. Pills and heat helped, but nothing fully relieved the pain.

Not that she'd get an operation based on one doctor's opinion. Zoe believed Dr. Wright, however, and expected a second and even third doctor to support her prognosis. But not yet. She couldn't bear to end all hope of having a family one day. She had already made an appointment with another ObGyn. But she knew it was only a matter time. Her doctor wouldn't have recommended the procedure if she hadn't been certain it was the only option left.

The pronouncement had been unexpected. Visiting the doctor yesterday afternoon, she'd been hoping for a new treatment, something that would work after five years of trying different medication.

But the miracle she hoped for hadn't appeared. Each month the pain grew worse. This month she'd been compelled to visit her doctor again. Too distraught to even think after the doctor's recommendation, she'd hopped in her car and driven to the Seagrass Point; to the cottage that had been in her family since her grandfather had been a little boy. It was a refuge, a haven. She sorely needed some time to come to terms with the change in her life.

Cottage was a bit of a misnomer—the old Victorian style house had five bedrooms and a kitchen large enough to feed a family of twenty. And there were usually that many in and out all summer long.

This stretch of beach on the Virginia side of Chesapeake Bay was privately owned. And in October it was practically deserted. The perfect place to hide away and come to terms with the realities of her life.

Zoe hadn't even told her twin yet. Chloe would insist on

driving out to join her as soon as she heard and at this moment, Zoe didn't want anyone around—not even the closest person to her in the world.

Her cell rang. It had rung a dozen times already today. Each time the chirpy ring startled her, bringing her out of her reverie for a few seconds. It lay on the counter in the kitchen. She could hear it but couldn't bring herself to leave her warm cocoon to walk inside to answer.

The relentless wave action of the sea mesmerized. The cool breeze chilled her cheeks. Tucked inside the warm quilt, getting up would mean being enveloped in the cold until she went inside. Maybe she'd just stay huddled in the quilt forever.

The phone went quiet. No one knew where she was. She'd phoned in to the office after she'd left the doctor's office and told her assistant she'd be out for a couple of days. Not stopping to check in with any of her family or friends, she'd driven straight to the beach. Sooner or later she'd have to call someone or they'd all worry. But not yet.

The phone rang again. For a moment Zoe thought it sounded angry. She smiled for the first time since seeing the doctor yesterday. Ring tones didn't sound angry. They just played whatever ring tone was set. Sighing, she rose and went inside. Her cramps were manageable, but she hunched over slightly. It was most likely Jedidiah Callahan—Cal for short—she could tell by the intense vibes winging their way unseen. Her boss didn't do things by half measures. If he decided he needed to speak to her, she'd better answer or who knew what he'd do next.

She grabbed the phone.

"Yes?"

The door hadn't latched behind her and the wind whipped

it wide-open, slamming it against the wall. Zoe winced as the cold air whirled around the kitchen.

"Where the heck are you and why isn't the Schribner folder where I think it ought to be?" Cal growled.

"I'm taking a couple of days off and the folder is with Ginny, ask her," she replied almost in the same snarl as she slammed the door shut. She was not in the mood to placate her boss. She had her own problem at the moment.

"And when I take time off from work, I'm not supposed to be working. You have a building full of employees, get one of them to find your blasted folder."

The silence on the other end lasted only a second. Then the silky tones of one trying to sooth a fractious child came over the line.

"Are you sick? It's not like you to miss work at all, much less without any warning."

She took a deep breath. Her private life was just that. She wasn't best friends with her boss though they had worked together for years. The longer she worked there, the more she and Cal meshed. He'd bounce ideas off her. She'd bring up situations that were beyond her for his input.

For a moment she wished she could confide in him. He was good at problem solving. But close as they were at work, they'd kept their personal lives private.

"I'll be back in a couple of days. You can manage until then."

Zoe disconnected and then turned off the phone. She'd have to call her sister soon. Once she came to terms with things, she'd want Chloe's advice. But in the meantime, she wanted to hole up and not talk to anyone—especially her sister.

Not that she was envious of her twin precisely. Okay, maybe she was just a little.

Chloe and Gabe married five years ago. They lived in a lovely apartment near Dupont Circle in the District of Columbia. Both successful in their respective professions, they traveled often, frequently to exotic locations. Sometimes trips were connected with Gabe's work as a troubleshooter for a tech company. Other times just for fun.

The only person Chloe loved as much as her twin was her husband. And once in a while Zoe almost wished he hadn't come along. Almost, but not really. Her sister was blissfully happy in her marriage and that was what Zoe envied.

If Zoe had married five years ago, she'd have children by now. Sometimes she wondered why Chloe didn't. The answer to the question—they weren't ready—seemed vague. But she'd never pushed for more. Everyone had their own timing.

Part of a large family, Zoe had always planned on having a large family of her own. She loved holidays and birthdays with her family. The closeness, the love, the feeling there was always someone there for her. She had deliberately sought to build a successful career before settling down to marriage and a family. Now it looked as if time had run out.

She dropped the quilt across one of the wooden chairs that surrounded the large plank kitchen table. Maybe she'd fix something to eat. If she had more energy, she'd go out to one of the local restaurants where the crab cakes were melt-in-your-mouth good. Or try one of the fish grills that dotted the town of Baden Harbor. But not tonight. She'd just heat up some soup and make toast. She wasn't hungry, but practical enough to know she needed to eat.

Things would look better in the morning, as her

grandmother always said.

Zoe didn't know how, but she hoped so.

Jedidiah Callahan carefully replaced the phone, stunned at the reaction of his normally cool-headed senior analyst. Zoe had worked for him for the last five years. He'd only seen her angry enough to yell twice. What set this episode off?

He thought back over the last couple of days. He hadn't been more difficult to work with than normal. So that wasn't it.

In fact, if asked, he'd have said they had a great relationship. She stood up to him when she thought he was wrong. Something other employees could learn. She voiced her feelings about projects, sometimes pinpointing exactly what was missing. And he relied on her more than any of the other analysts to give him sound advice.

He rose and went down the hall and peered into her office. Tidy as always. She was neat beyond normal, he often thought; while his own desk was piled high with folders and printouts and reports. Zoe loved order, spreadsheets and tons of data to analyze. He counted on her to have the information he wanted when he wanted it. He was used to Zoe being there whenever he needed her. This wasn't like her at all. Now he'd have to find Ginny and see if she could locate the file. And maybe give him some information on what was up with Zoe.

The younger woman was diligently typing a report from one of the field agents. She looked up when Cal stopped at her desk and almost grimaced before giving him an artificial smile.

"What can I do for you?" she asked.

"I'm looking for the Schribner folder," he said.

"Oh, dear. I remember seeing that. Just hold on a sec and let me remember where."

Ginny jumped up and began to rummage through the stacks of folders on her desk. It resembled his, but there the similarity ended. Jedidiah knew exactly where every piece of paper was on his. Ginny was still rummaging through piles.

"Zoe was working on it, making sure everything was up today because you're meeting with them soon and she wanted you to have every iota of intel at your fingertips," Ginny mumbled as she rifled through yet another stack of folders. "She called in yesterday and had me get it from her office. It's here. Wait a sec."

Cal took a deep breath, trying not to let his frustration spill over. His first tendency was to snap and then make amends, but he wouldn't do that today. He had more control over his behavior. But he didn't have much patience in the best of times and this was not the best of times. Blast it, why had Zoe taken off at this juncture? He needed her.

"Here it is." Ginny beamed with success and handed him the thick folder.

He took it and walked away. At least one thing had gone right today. Where the heck was Zoe? She hadn't requested vacation time. She wasn't claiming sick leave. Was something wrong with someone in her family?

He didn't know much about her personal life, just that her family came from Maryland and she had more brothers and sisters than anyone else he knew. Most of whom also worked in the District of Columbia.

He returned to his desk and opened the folder. His curiosity over Zoe and her odd behavior wouldn't let him focus on the material therein. If she were sick, wouldn't she have said something? Normally he knew her schedule as well as he knew his own—and vice versa.

Cal tried her phone again. The not-in-service message came on. He uttered a brief expletive and hung up.

Ten minutes later Cal closed the Schribner folder and rose. His security firm specialized in keeping people safe, especially when traveling to dangerous locales. The agents assigned the Schribner account could handle things. Cal would check on Zoe one more time and then call it a day.

Maybe put in some time at the gym. The exercise tired him out enough to sleep at night.

Though the nightmares still struck without warning.

He'd given Zoe a ride home a few times over the years. Her apartment building was out near Key Bridge. He'd never been inside. Entering the building a short time later Cal noticed it was as nondescript as most modern buildings. The elevator was quiet and quickly rose to her floor. Ringing the doorbell brought no response. He leaned against the door to listen. He heard nothing. He tried her phone again. No service. Where was she?

After eating her soup, Zoe perused the books in the shelves. She'd read all of them, a couple more than once. Light summertime reading, none would hold her attention today. She considered going to bed, but it was too early—though darkness had fallen. Sighing softly, she went to the cottage phone and called her sister. Time to tell Chloe what was going on.

Zoe felt marginally better after their conversation. Her twin had been as shocked with the news as Zoe had and wanted to jump right in the car and drive down to the beach, but Zoe had convinced her talking on the phone was good enough.

So then her sister had come up with a dozen of different scenarios all in which Zoe was miraculously cured.

When they'd exhausted those options, they settled into a heart-to-heart.

"Mostly I wanted a family one day, like ours," Zoe told her. "Can you imagine life without all the kids running around and grandparents and aunts and uncles?"

"Actually, I can. That's what Gabe and I have."

"But if you wanted children, at least you're married. I'm not even seeing anyone," Zoe said.

"That's because you're too involved with Cal."

"I'm not involved with my boss," she denied quickly.

Immediately his image came to mind—tall with dark brown hair and a body to die for. He turned the heads of lots of women, but never settled on one. She pictured his concentration at work. The serious focus of his eyes on the reports. Running his hands through his hair when frustrated. His laughter if they took a break and ordered pizza while staying late because of some crisis.

"Not that way, silly. I mean too caught up in work. You're more of a workaholic than Gabe is. If Cal says he needs you, there you are. I'm surprised you're not at work right now," Chloe said.

"Now you're being silly. I'm not there all the time."

Though she did work more closely with Cal than any other analyst. But that was because he needed her.

"I enjoy what I do. I thought I could have my career for a little longer and then think about getting married and starting a family," Zoe said pensively.

"Well, you'd enjoy finding someone with lots in common and falling in love. Set some boundaries—let Cal know you can only work for eight hours a day, not twenty-four. You have time. Just not as much as you always thought. The doctor didn't say get into hospital next week."

"She did say soon. There's always so much to do at the office. The business keeps expanding as Cal's reputation grows. He's really providing a terrific service with fabulous results."

"Great, he can hire some more help if business is booming. Let him deal with that. Your next assignment is to find a husband, get married and start that family," Chloe said.

Zoe sighed. "That sounds so calculating. These days a woman doesn't really have to be married to have a baby."

She always thought she'd fall in love like her twin, with a man who was perfect for her. One who also wanted a large family. Was that a pipe dream?

"You're not thinking of a sperm bank?" Chloe asked, the incredulity coming clearly across the phone line.

"No. I can't imagine raising a child alone. Wait, before you say a word, I know you'll be there for me as will the rest of the family. But I want my baby to have a father. Can you imagine our lives without Dad? I'm not sure that would be fair to a child, to deliberately bring him or her into the world with no father. I mean it's one thing if something happens, but to start out that way, I'm not sure."

"You have five brothers, each would be a perfect father figure. Gabe would as well."

"It's not the same thing as having your very own. So even if I don't marry the father, I want a man who'll be a part of the child's life forever."

"Women who fall in love and get married don't even get that guarantee," Chloe said.

"I want it anyway."

Her sister thought for a moment. "I guess it's worth a

shot. Maybe you'll fall for a man and get married and end up with a dozen kids."

"Or maybe find someone I really like, who is good father material and wants a baby without all the ties and commitment of marriage," Zoe said thoughtfully. "I mean, how much do I really want to be tied down? I'd be there for the baby, but I still want to work. What if a husband didn't want that?"

She didn't even want to think about giving up her career.

"Ties and commitment are necessary with a child," Chloe said. "And you're strong enough to stand up for yourself married or not. It's not an either or decision."

"You're right. Still, I'd have to choose a daddy carefully, whatever else happened."

Zoe rose early the next morning. The sun was peeping above the horizon, below the clouds that were rapidly dissipating. She hoped it'd be a better day than yesterday, but the pain that woke her didn't hold much promise. Staying another day meant she'd need to visit one of the grocery stores. The canned goods that stocked the cottage cupboards didn't offer the variety she craved.

But she couldn't face that now. Groaning slightly, she curled up in a ball.

Waking an hour later, she felt awful. She made it to the bathroom and her pills. After a few minutes, she headed back for bed when someone knocked on the front door. She debated letting them stay there, she longed for bed. But curiosity more than anything won out and she went to the door.

Opening it, Zoe stared at Cal Callahan standing on the porch, towering over her. His expression was impossible to read. He wore a suit, the tie loosened. He hadn't shaved yet that morning and the shadow of his beard made him look more rugged and masculine than normal.

"What are you doing here?" she asked.

"I came to see you."

"How did you find the place?"

"Interesting story, that," he said, glancing at her attire. "You getting up or going to bed?"

She pulled the lapels of the warm fleece robe closer and shook her head.

"Today isn't a good day, Cal."

She began to push the door shut.

He held it open easily and stepped inside.

"You look like you need some help."

"More than you can give."

"Meaning?"

He studied her closely. Zoe was conscious she hadn't even washed her face that morning. Her hair probably looked like the wreck of the *Hesperus*. She hated not projecting her normal cool demeanor. But at the moment, none of it mattered.

"I went to your sister's home and she gave me directions to here. Which seems like a good thing, now. I didn't know you two were twins. That was a shock."

Zoe nodded wondering how much longer she could remain upright. She always kept her family life separate from work.

"I'm surprised you even knew I had a sister, much less where to find her."

"She's listed as the person to notify in case of emergency."

"And you count this as an emergency?"

He looked at her. "You tell me. Why aren't you in bed? You look terrible."

"Gee, thanks. Actually I need to be."

He scooped her up and asked which way. Zoe almost protested, but it felt so good to relinquish control for just a second. And being off her feet eased some of the discomfort—or the pills were beginning to work.

"Talk to me," he said as he walked up the stairs to the bedroom she used.

Zoe didn't want to let him know everything, but she did owe him an explanation. Her flight had been unlike her and he had a right to know if it would happen again. She wondered if anything else would be so devastating she'd immediately flee to the comfort of the family sea cottage.

"Two heads are better than one at solving problems," he said.

He gently put her on the bed and once she covered herself with the spread, sat on the edge of the mattress.

"It won't happen again," she said.

"What happened and won't again?" he asked.

"I won't leave so unexpectedly like this time. It was a private emergency."

"Hey, Protection, Inc. is good in emergencies. We have strategic planning down to an art. I doubt there are many things we can't handle. Besides, you help me in brainstorming solution, let's try this one."

She almost smiled. Cal was so proud of the company—and rightly so. Their success rate was terrific. It was becoming synonymous with high end security in the capital. The firm was constantly hiring new agents as it expanded. One department did nothing but vet new hires. Cal made security as sacred as apple pie.

"Unfortunately the company can't help in this situation," she said.

"Try me," he invited.

He looked rock solid, firm and dependable. She knew he was as honest as anyone she'd met. And he had an aura of competency that was evident at first glance. Wind had ruffled his dark hair when he walked to the cottage from his car, giving him an almost boyish look. She blinked. She'd met him when he'd been in his thirties. There was nothing boyish about the hard-as-nails man who drove Protection, Inc. He was right, she and he had worked together for years. Might as well share this little bit.

"All right." She'd take him up on his challenge. "I found out yesterday I need to have a hysterectomy and I always wanted a family. If I don't do something soon, I can forget about ever having a baby."

Cal didn't move, didn't even blink, but Zoe knew she'd startled him.

"It's a female problem and getting worse. My doctor recommended I get the operation soon—like before next month. Where does that fall in Protection's purview?"

Unexpectedly he reached out and brushed her hair away from her cheek. Zoe was shocked at the awareness that shot through her. This was Cal, her boss, mentor and friend. She refused to hear Chloe's words echo in her mind about being too involved with Cal.

"Not one of our more usual situations," he murmured.

"You wanted to know," she reminded him.

She respected him more than anyone she knew. She often marveled at the dangerous situations he was able to defuse. But even Cal couldn't pull miracles out of a hat.

"Don't worry, this is my problem, not yours. I don't see it has much of a solution—much less a quick one."

"You work for me so it becomes my problem," Cal said.

"I'm coming to grips with the situation," she said, feeling awkward discussing it with her boss.

Their relationship had always been business. Now he was in her bedroom. He'd touched her in a way not consistent with being her boss.

"But it isn't going away," he said.

"Sooner or later, I need that operation. I just wanted to have a baby first."

Her voice cracked a little. Zoe took a deep breath. She was done with crying.

"Ironic," he murmured.

"What is?"

"Nothing. No boyfriend ready to step up to the plate?" he asked.

She shook her head and shot him a look.

"When do I have time to date and build some kind of relationship? In case you didn't know, my boss is a slaver driver," she teased, trying to lighten the mood.

He didn't need to shoulder her problems.

"Hey, whatever it takes to get the job done."

"What it takes is two or three people to keep up with you," she retorted.

"You've never complained," he said.

"You know how exciting the work can be. I love it. But I think I'll need to make some changes. I hate to hit the singles bars, but if I want a family—and I do—I could have left it too late. Still, I have to try."

He touched her shoulder, the awareness building again.

"I have a few friends I could introduce you to. I know

Mark Wyatt was married for a while and liked being married."

"What happened?"

"His wife didn't, apparently. Anyway, they split about a year ago. He might be right what you're looking for. He's around my age, no children yet. Maybe he'd be interested."

"That hardly sounds romantic," she said.

"Hey, you want romance, you need to take your time. You want a sperm donor, you take what you can get."

"Cal, I can't believe you said that. It sounds horrible. I don't just want a donor, I want someone to make a baby with and then raise that baby together, going to school functions, family gatherings. I'd like to get married if I can find the right man, but if that's not in the cards, I still want a father who will be there when the child graduates college and gets married and makes us grandparents."

"What time warp are you coming from?" he asked.

"What do you mean? That's not so much to ask."

"In this day and age it is. Who do you know who's still married when their kids graduate college?"

"My parents for one. My grandparents are all alive, all four. There has only been one divorce in our family in three generations," she said. "But marriage isn't necessary. Mostly I want someone committed to being a dad. Someone who will love our child as much as I will."

"Weigh the chances and the parameters you have to work with. See what level of comfort you can stand and go for it. It may be single motherhood is the cost of a child."

"I guess I have some serious thinking to do."

"Want something to eat while doing that serious thinking?"

"Can you cook?"

Zoe knew he could order pizza with the best of them, but she'd never had a reason to know if he could cook. It gave a different dimension to him.

"I can manage eggs and toast," he said.

"I think there's only dry cereal and oatmeal."

"I'll manage, you rest."

He stood up and walked out of the bedroom.

Zoe breathed a sigh of relief. Cal was too energetic for the way she felt. She meant what she said—she had some serious decisions to make. Could she find someone to fall in love with on demand? Cal already promised to introduce her to an eligible man. Her sisters would, she knew. Some friends had been trying to fix her up for years, but she'd always had her work. And Cal—as Chloe said.

Zoe didn't want to return to work. She wanted to stay at the cottage and gather her resources a bit before returning home. Yet if Cal was going to introduce her to someone he thought she might like, maybe the sooner done the better. She hoped this month's bout of pain vanished soon.

Cal brought up oatmeal and tea. He sat beside her and matched her spoonful for spoonful. She thought it funny he'd eat so plainly, and drink tea when she knew he devoured coffee all day long.

A couple of times during the meal, she caught Cal studying her. Zoe wanted to squirm under his intense regard, but did her best to appear unconcerned propped up against the headboard. The pills were beginning to take effect and she felt marginally better.

She appreciated his taking care of her. She never expected

that. Fighting terrorists or kidnappers, yes, taking care of a sick friend—no. Showed she really didn't know all she could about him.

"Are you tabulating every flaw to pass on to your friend?" she finally asked.

"No, I'm mentally listing all the attributes I think will have him falling over himself to date you. You're prettier than I noticed before."

She felt a spurt of amusement. "Thanks, I think."

"Well, we don't have that kind of relationship. I never noticed how pretty you are."

"You have your own bevy of female companions," she said. "I bet they're all beautiful."

She'd seen several over the years—always model thin and glam.

"The old adage about beauty only being skin deep still applies."

He looked down at his tea, slowly lifting the cup to sip.

Zoe wondered what she might have said to cause that pensive—no almost *pained* look. Had he and a girlfriend just broken up? She tried to remember the last woman in his life. Suzette or Suzanne or something like that. Occasionally she heard him talking to her on the phone. Cal also kept his personal life out of the office.

She suddenly realized she knew very little about her boss beyond the day-to-day operations of the business. How odd. After working closely together for so long, they should know more about each other.

"What does this Mark look like?" she asked.

"He's about my height. Has sandy color hair. He's really

interested in football, follows major league teams all season long. Goes to the same gym I go to."

Zoe wondered if she'd like that. She knew something about football, with five brothers, how could she not? But she wasn't a passionate fan.

"What else?"

"He's in advertising, doing very well."

She wrinkled her nose.

"Not something you like?"

"Too much cajoling people to buy stuff they don't need."

"Part of the economy."

"I guess. Is he from Washington?" she asked.

"Not originally. From the Midwest somewhere, but has lived in DC for a dozen years or more. I think he went to Georgetown University and just stayed. You two would have great kids together."

"I'll reserve judgment until I meet the man," she murmured. "Did you get the Schribner file?"

The conversation changed to business and Zoe and Cal fell into their familiar pattern of discussing clients and the various needs, who would be good to handle certain aspects and the shortfalls of one of the newer recruits.

By the time their meal was finished, Zoe felt better, physically and mentally. Talking with Cal pulled her back into the work arena and had her temporarily forget the ticking clock. She'd give anything to be normal, but since she wasn't, maybe she should take a page from Cal's book and find a way around the problem.

Once breakfast was finished, she expected him to take off. Instead he said he'd hang out for a while and let her sleep.

Whenever she awoke, he was nearby, offering tea or food. Somewhere during the day, he'd gone out and bought groceries. Lunch was more substantial than breakfast and dinner was almost a feast.

Cal left after dinner but promised to return the next day, despite Zoe's protests. It was over an hour's drive from DC to Seagrass Point. He didn't need to be wasting his time. She'd be back home before long.

The next day, Zoe felt better. She'd made it through another month. She wasn't surprised when he showed up again. He usually only said what he meant, and he had said he'd return.

"You don't have to wait on me, I'll be fine now," she said at breakfast, eaten downstairs this morning after a quick shower and clean clothes. She still felt awkward at Cal's newfound concern for her.

"There are things waiting at the office," he said, slowly.

"Then you should be there, not here. I'll be in tomorrow for sure."

"I can wait," he said. "Give you a ride back."

"No need. I have my car. I have to drive it back anyway."

"If you're sure?"

"I am."

She walked him out to his car a short time later, wondering if any neighbors were around to see the sleek black sports car, which was a testimony to his success. Zoe rarely saw the car without wishing she could drive it, just once.

She'd love to ride up to her parents' home when the entire family was gathered. Her brother Sean especially would turn green with envy.

"I'll be in tomorrow," she said.

Cal nodded and said, "Just don't leave me to Ginny for long."

"She's not that bad. You frighten her," Zoe said. "Be nice to her, she'll do fine."

"I'm always nice," he said as he prepared to leave.

He touched her shoulder. Zoe resisted the impulse to lean against him for strength. She wanted to keep their relationship normal. She couldn't take any more distractions at this point.

Zoe watched as he drove away. Nice was not the word she'd use to describe her boss. But sometimes he could be kind. She walked back out to the beach, wishing the sun was shining brightly and children were playing on the sand. Instead she had the lonely cry of the gulls to keep her company on a blustery day.

Cal drove back to the city reviewing the business awaiting his attention. Maybe he hadn't needed to seek out Zoe, but he'd wanted to see for himself that she was all right. Finding out she wasn't had shaken him. She'd always seemed indestructible. He never remembered her sick before.

These past two days had shown a vulnerability that startled him. And brought out protective instincts he hadn't known he had.

Meeting her sister had also been a surprise. She looked exactly like Zoe. At first, he'd thought his assistant had gotten married and planned to quit her job. He'd been relieved and intrigued to discover the twin connection. What other surprises would he discover if he hung around her longer?

The revelation that she might not be able to have children—and longed to have them—had been another. Not that they'd ever discussed lifelong dreams, but she was devoted to work. Of course she had a private life. She didn't go into hibernation at night and reappear at the office the next morning.

Yet he felt he was seeing Zoe in three dimension for the first time.

Life was so unfair. He'd known that since he'd been a small boy bewildered when he learned of the death of his mother and his father's abandonment. But it still astounded him sometimes.

Like now. Zoe wanted a baby so badly and had no one to make one with. While Suzanne had been pregnant with their child and ended its chance before it was born.

Chapter Two

Zoe arrived at work early Thursday morning. She had her coffee in hand and was prioritizing her phone calls when Cal entered her small office and looked at her.

"I hoped you'd be back today. How are you feeling?"

"Back to normal, thank you."

She felt awkward and embarrassed remembering him seeing her at her worst and preparing her meals.

"Good. Mark's meeting me for lunch. I thought the three of us could go together."

"Today?" she asked, surprised Cal had acted so quickly in lining someone up.

She half thought he'd been giving her lip service.

"No time like the present. Mark will be here at noon."

With that he disappeared down the hall.

The phone rang and Zoe's day began.

As noon approached, Zoe grew more and more nervous. She'd never met anyone before with the deliberate intent of seeing if they could hit it off enough to get involved. How far would it go—to marriage?

She thought when the right man came along she'd recognize him immediately and be swept off her feet. Now she felt like some of the man-hungry women she'd read about

out for only a meal ticket. Only in her case it was a baby ticket. Was she wrong to try for a family? She'd miss so much from life if she never had a child of her own.

She made a good income. She didn't need a man to support her. But she did need a man if she wanted a baby before it was too late. One who would be a good father—and loving husband?

Cal and a tall man with sandy hair entered her office promptly at noon. She looked up and smiled at them both, feeling like an actress getting ready to go on stage who couldn't remember her lines. The visitor smiled easily when Cal introduced him.

"Join us for lunch," Cal said as if it wasn't already planned.

"Thanks, I'd like to."

She pretended she didn't see the surprised look Mark had given Cal. This was never going to work.

Zoe felt awkward at the lunch table. For one wild moment she considered refusing when Cal had issued the invitation, but her boss had gone to all this trouble for her, she had to hold up her end.

Soon, however, the awkwardness began to ease when Mark proved to be entertaining and personable. Probably needed to be for his job, she thought skeptically. She couldn't help compare the two men. Cal was dark, quiet, intense. Mark had a sunnier disposition and seemed interested in her. Maybe they would hit it off.

When lunch was finished, Cal excused himself—to be available for an important phone call due from Europe.

"For the first time since I've known him, his timing is superb," Mark said when Cal left.

"Oh?" Zoe asked.

"I was hoping I'd get a moment alone with you. I'd like to invite you to dinner, if you're free."

"I'd love to," she replied. Had a script been written out, it couldn't have gone better.

"Tonight?" Mark asked.

"Terrific," she said, smiling.

Her heart didn't skip a beat. There was no sense of weightlessness or flutter of excitement. But Mark was entertaining and maybe feelings would develop. She couldn't expect love at first sight. That was a fantasy in books.

Cal was in a meeting when she returned to the office. She wanted to let him know about her dinner date, but couldn't leave a message with his secretary. She hoped the cryptic note would clue him in.

The afternoon flew by. Cal stopped at her desk at one point, on his way to meet with some of the operatives.

"So?" he said, holding up the note she'd left.

"Date tonight," she said.

He nodded and moved on. Zoe watched him walk away. She was disappointed he didn't want to know more. He'd set it up, wasn't he curious? Sighing, she turned back to the analysis she was working on. He'd know soon enough if she and Mark would make a match of it.

Her phone rang.

"Zoe," she answered, glancing at the time. Another hour or so and she'd take off.

"Hey, thought you were coming to see me when you got back from the cottage," her sister said without preamble.

"It was late last night and I came to work early this morning."

"Obviously. I called before but you were busy. You doing

okay?" Chloe asked.

"I'm hanging in there, if that's what you wanted to know."

"Feeling okay?"

"Much better."

Zoe sighed softly. It was a day-by-day thing at the time of her period. The rest of the time her life seemed normal.

"I've been thinking what you need is a social life to find some man to fall for," Chloe said.

"I'm ahead of you there, I have a date tonight."

"Really, who with?"

"Cal introduced me to one of his friends."

"Why would he do that?" Chloe asked.

"I told him about the situation."

"He came to the cottage, didn't he? I thought he might when he almost browbeat me into giving out where you were. Were you okay with that?"

"Yes, that was fine. He listened to my tale of woe and came up with this idea—meet his friend who used to be married and wants to be married again. Maybe we'll hit it off. We all had lunch together today and Mark asked me to dinner tonight."

She didn't tell Chloe about Cal's help for two days. Her sister would jump to erroneous conclusions.

"Fast worker. How are you feeling about that?"

"He seems nice."

"Yuck, the kiss of death. No one wants to be nice. If he's only nice, he's not for you."

Zoe laughed.

"Don't be silly. Of course I want a nice man for a husband. What—do you think I should have someone not nice?"

"How would you describe your boss?"

Zoe went still for a moment. "Why?"

"I figured you would fall for someone like him. You and I are alike and he's the closest man to Gabe I know."

"He's nothing like your husband."

"Maybe not superficially, but they both have that rock-hard center, they know their way around the world and give me the feeling of being able to take on anything—and come out the winner."

Zoe nodded, then realized her sister couldn't see her.

"I guess. But I'm definitely not his type. His latest girlfriend could be a super model. Thin, beautiful and sophisticated."

"You're pretty and sophisticated," Chloe said.

Zoe laughed. "I noticed you left out the thin part. But I'm not in her league, not that I want to be. Cal's not for me. Anyway, I'll let you know more about Mark after dinner tonight. Gotta go."

She hung up and returned to her task. Her and Cal? Where did Chloe come up with such an idea? She refused to give that a moment's thought. They were work colleagues—nothing more.

It was after eleven by the time Zoe returned home. Dinner had been at one of the "in" restaurants in Washington. Even on a Thursday evening it had been crowded. Mark had reserved a table so there'd been virtually no wait. Zoe wondered how he'd managed that.

She kicked off her shoes and went into the kitchen. Putting the kettle on, she got tea from the cupboard. A cup of chamomile would help her relax. She yawned, feeling her cheek muscles protest. She couldn't remember the last time she'd smiled so much. Be polite, she could hear her mother's voice echoing throughout the night.

The phone rang. She went to answer, noticing the flashing light on her answering machine.

"So how did it go?" Cal asked when she answered.

Zoe was surprised to hear from him. Chloe she expected.

"All right."

"Only all right?"

"He's nice."

"But?"

"Does there have to be a but?" she asked, stalling. Mark was Cal's friend.

"Yes, with that lead-in, there does."

She hesitated a moment. It would serve no purpose to delay, time wouldn't change anything.

"He's nice and still hung up on his ex-wife. If I had to listen to another word about how he'd screwed up and how she'd been an angel only he hadn't seen it in time, I thought I would scream."

"The man has rocks for brains," Cal said. "Did he talk about her all night?"

"No. That's what is sort of sad. He'd talk about something, then end up talking about her. Once he'd realize he was doing that, he'd stop and try another topic, segueing back to his ex. I think he really wants to be over her, but he's not."

"Are you seeing him again?"

"No."

The silence stretched out for several seconds.

"Maybe I know someone else," Cal said slowly.

"Forget it. Chloe knows some men she says are right up

my alley. I'll see how I get along with them. It's my own fault. I love my job, you know that. I still should have done more about a social life before now."

"This was only the first day of your campaign."

"You make it sound like a war strategy."

It wasn't at all like she hoped. She pictured herself as happy as her twin when she fell in love. Now the entire thing sounded analytical and deliberate. Where was the happiness in all this? Was the price of a baby going to be too high?

"It is a kind of strategy. You need to find the right match."

"Mmm. It's early, I know, but what if I don't find someone I can even think of going to bed with?"

"Was that the real problem with Mark?"

She thought about it a moment.

"Yes. No matter what, I couldn't see myself getting intimate with the man."

"It was a first date," Cal said.

"I don't think that would change."

"You'll find someone. Let me know how your sister's friends work out. I have another couple of friends who are still single."

"Maybe they want to stay single like you," she said.

"You think I won't marry?"

"Cal, you're thirty-six years old and haven't come close to getting married yet. You date some of the world's most beautiful women. I think you're hard to please. And you have to admit, you spend a lot of time at work. Relationships take time to build and maintain."

"That doesn't mean I don't want a family—someday."

Zoe heard the kettle whistling. She walked into the kitchen and turned off the gas.

"Do you believe there are several people in the world a person could be equally happy with? Or that each of us only has one?"

"I haven't thought about it."

"I mean that one man for one woman sounds awfully chancy. What if they pass each other by? Would neither ever find happiness?" Zoe asked wistfully.

"You're getting too philosophical for tonight. Go to sleep and tomorrow see what your sister turns up."

"Goodnight," she said.

Zoe fixed her tea and went to the living room. Turning off the lights, she opened her drapes and gazed out over the lights of Washington. Sipping the warm beverage she thought about her evening. The highlight had been the conversation with Cal. What did that say about her chances of finding Mr. Right?

How odd her sister thought she should be on the lookout for someone like Cal. He was handsome in a very sexy way, if she let herself think about it. Mostly she considered him her boss. And she'd decided early in her tenure with Protection, Inc. not to become involved with a fellow employee. She'd heard of office romances gone bad. Her job had been too important to her to risk it.

For a moment she wondered what it'd be like to be romanced by Cal. Fleeting, at best. He had a different girlfriend every few months. She'd rather spend hours each week working with him, than be one in a long line of dates.

She finished her tea and went to bed. Tomorrow would provide new opportunities.

Saturday Zoe spent thoroughly cleaning her apartment. Not that it was messy, mostly dusty and needing some freshening. She wasn't home enough to clutter up things. Once done, she changed into clean jeans and a pink top and headed for her sister's. They had planning to do.

Chloe and Gabe had a luxury apartment near Dupont Circle, a neighborhood in Washington for young professionals, with outdoor cafés and a wide variety of ethnic restaurants. The shops were upscale and unique, a pleasure to browse through. Parking was a problem, so Zoe took a cab. Just as she arrived, it began to rain. So much for planning a quick walk and coffee at one of the cafés, she thought.

When Zoe reached her sister's apartment, Chloe was waiting. She threw open the door and reached out to hug her.

"Come in. Gabe's away for a few days, so it's just us. Isn't the weather a bummer. I thought we could take a walk and talk."

"My thoughts exactly."

They grinned at each other. They'd shared that bond all their lives.

"I can order in. A caramel macchiato for you, right?" Chloe asked.

"And you'll have the double cap," Zoe said, taking off her jacket. "Where is Gabe off to this time?"

"Brussels. There's some big NATO event going and they're using super computers and he's needed to make sure they run with no glitches."

"And you didn't want to go?" Zoe asked.

"Not this time. I have a big deal about to close. I want to be here for that."

Chloe was in real estate, selling homes in an area of Washington that catered to embassy personnel and members of Congress.

"Let me order the coffees and then you and I need to discuss this situation. I can't believe we didn't know this would become a crisis. Surely something else can be done to help you," Chloe said.

Zoe filled her in on all the doctor had to say.

"There's no guarantee I can even get pregnant. But if I want a chance at a baby of my own, I need to at least try," she ended.

"Did the doctor give you a time limit?" Chloe asked.

"No, but each month the pain gets worse. It must be getting worse, this month is the first time I've missed work."

"Maybe you didn't tell me the full extent of everything."

Zoe shrugged. "It doesn't matter. I guess it's a matter of how long I can hold out. Dr. Wright wanted to schedule the op at my last visit."

"Hold on a little longer. Let me tell you about this friend of mine in the office. He's about our age and never been married. So no ex-wife to bore you with."

"Do you think he's interested in marriage and kids?"

"With the right woman, of course."

Zoe didn't take her sister's assertion to heart. But what did she have to lose? If he turned out to be the man of her heart, she'd be forever grateful.

"So tell me more about him," Zoe said.

Cal threw his pencil on the desk and rose, pacing around the office. He couldn't concentrate. The normal appeal of the job was missing. Saturdays usually allowed him to catch up. He was too distracted to concentrate. This was going on too long. He wasn't sleeping well and knew he had to get beyond the grief he held for a baby he'd never known.

He went to the window. The rain slanted down, blurring

his view. It looked cold. As cold as he felt every time he thought about Suzanne and her unconscionable act.

Comparing her with Zoe came naturally these days. One woman casually and callously ended a baby's life before it even had a chance. The other was doing all she could to be able to have a baby that she'd cherish all its life. Why hadn't fate denied Suzanne a pregnancy and granted an easy time for his analyst?

Talking with Zoe at the shore had reaffirmed his faith in women. She wanted a baby desperately. He'd heard all his life how his mother had so longed for a child she'd risked her own life, and lost. Those were the kind of women that kept the species going. He wished he could do something for Zoe. He was in the business of providing solutions, why couldn't he find one for her?

He turned and looked at the stack of folders on his desk. Maps lined one wall, on sliding bars to move in and out of the forefront. He'd built up a good security business over the last twelve years. The need continued unabated and the company was growing to meet demand.

But Suzanne's heinous act had knocked him off his original course. He'd thought he'd find a woman to admire, respect and want to build a life with. She'd provide him with children who could inherit the business, make his uncle a grandfather. Someone to spend holidays with, share celebrations and downturns.

He wanted to offer more for any children he may have than he'd been given. Not that his uncle didn't do his best. Part of the reason Cal pushed so hard to make a success was for a future generation.

That had ended before it even had a chance. Anger at

Suzanne flared all over again. How could she have had an abortion just to keep from stretch marks and morning sickness? They'd used protection every time. Only something had happened. There could have been choices, except she'd had the abortion before telling him she was pregnant.

He'd spent as much time and anguish over her as he wanted. She was out of his life. He hadn't dated anyone in the last ten months. He'd been gifted with keen insight in security measures. Why hadn't that extended to Suzanne and her intentions? He fisted his hand again, wanting to hit out, assuage the thirst for revenge. There was nothing he could do to change the past, only mourn the outcome.

He only wished the grief at the loss of the baby would fade as quickly as the feelings he once thought he had for Suzanne had vanished. Life was unfair, as his uncle often said. Zoe longed for a baby. He should have slept with her if there was to be a mistake, not coldhearted Suzanne.

The phone rang. Glad for the distraction, Cal answered on the second ring.

"Mark here. I made a hash of things," his friend said.

Cal leaned against the desk.

"What are you talking about?"

He had a good idea, but didn't want his friend to know his part of connecting him with Zoe, or that he'd already spoken with Zoe.

"I took Zoe out to dinner the other night and spent the entire time talking about Wendy. How dumb can one man be?"

Cal thought about his own connection with Suzanne and how he'd misjudged her.

"Join the club. It's a man thing—act dumb around women."

Mark sighed. "Think so?"

"What happened?"

"Nothing. I took her home. She smiled all night long but never gave any indication she wanted a kiss or anything. So I thought I'd play it cool. Then I called her last night and only got her answering machine. I've called twice today. She never answers. Guess I need to take the hint, huh?"

"Give her a day or two and try again. If she doesn't take that call, then give up," Cal suggested.

He knew Zoe didn't want more dates with Mark, but he hated his friend sounding so down.

"Maybe. Or maybe I need to get my act together first and get over Wendy. I thought I was ready, obviously not."

The two talked for a short time. When he was off the phone later, Cal considered himself lucky he'd been able to get over Suzanne. He hoped he never became so caught up with another person he couldn't function any better than Mark if the relationship ended.

He picked up a folder and rose. He'd stop by Zoe's desk to see if she were in. She often worked on Saturdays. He shook his head, what was he doing—he didn't need to see her today. Monday would be time enough. Only he continued heading toward her office.

Zoe wasn't at her desk.

He was about to leave when he saw a piece of paper on the floor near her printer. Unlike Zoe to have anything out of place. He crossed and picked it up to place on her desk. Glancing at it Cal was startled to find it was a checklist of some kind—for a father for her baby.

He put down his folder, nudged her door closed and sat behind her desk, his eyes taking in the list of attributes she wanted in the father of her baby.

Athletic (no sedentary lifestyle)

Knowledgeable about many things (to better teach our child)

Interested in childhood events (school plays, field trips, prom)

Strong interest in education (college)

Interest in finer things (Art galleries, Smithsonian, Kennedy Center)

Sense of family (there until adult at least)

Cal read all the items on the list; some were a puzzle to him, but most were clear. Zoe was listing criteria for the father of her baby. Cal gave a sardonic chuckle. How many men would relish being judged on criteria listed instead of on themselves or a spark of attraction between them?

Curious, he began to jot notes beside each. He spent time behind his desk, but he didn't consider his life sedentary. He worked out at the gym, liked to ski in winter, sail in summer. And being out in the field kept a man busy providing the needed protection his clients demanded.

It was after seven by the time he finished. An exercise in getting into Zoe's mind, he thought as he balled up the paper and tossed it into the trash. He thought he knew how she thought from their working together. But her list surprised him. Not the fact she had a list; as long as he'd known her, she was always jotting down lists. But the various aspects she considered important were the surprise.

Nowhere did he see anything that applied to a lover or mate for her. Was she so caught up in a baby, she discounted herself?

He took his folder and left. The offices were silent.

Everyone working today had left except the night crew manning the monitors. He passed that large room, glanced in through the glass walls and noted people competently carrying out their assigned tasks. He knew everyone there, but only in a business sense.

The same way he knew Zoe. But the glimpse into her personal life intrigued him. Especially after thinking about her criteria. Why wasn't she looking for something for herself? Or maybe there was a page two and he hadn't seen. The thought almost had him turning around to try to get into her computer to search. But that would be an invasion of privacy, and Cal had a strong sense of right and wrong. It bumped the limits reading the paper from the floor. He'd never deliberately go into her files without her permission.

But it didn't stop him from speculating what she'd want in a lover.

He had never thought about her in that light. For a moment he could picture her cheeks flushed with passion, her eyes sparkling and her smile seductive. It wouldn't take much imagination to see her on a bed, with that glossy brown hair spread out around her and her lips parted in temptation.

Sunday morning Zoe slept in—at least for her. She rose at eight and took a quick shower. The day loomed endlessly. Last night's date had been another bust. Maybe there was a reason for her not being part of a couple—she was too picky. But she couldn't help it. She wanted the best man possible to father her baby. Was it her fault she couldn't find one? Mark hadn't appealed to her on a basic level. Not to mention he was still hung up on his ex-wife.

Peter from Chloe's office sounded too immature himself to be considered as a father. For some men having children caused them to grow up. In this case, Zoe suspected she would find rivalry between Peter and a baby. Not her ideal situation.

And somewhere she had to add sex appeal. So far the thought of kissing any of the men hadn't held any appeal. How could she get naked with them?

After a hasty breakfast, she put on warm wool slacks and a sweater. She'd run by the office for a little while and make sure she had all the latest data for the head of that African country's visit next month. Not a big player in world politics, nonetheless she wanted to make sure his visit to the nation's capital went without a hitch. And one never knew where fanatics lurked.

Entering the office a short time later, she went right to work. It was almost noon by the time she was ready to take a break. Maybe she'd get a sandwich at the deli up the street and study some of the men there. She felt as if she was becoming skewed in her thinking. Now everything revolved around men, men, men.

Glancing around as she rose, she noticed a ball of paper in her otherwise empty wastepaper basket. She never did that. Curious, she pulled it out and smoothed it open. It was one of her lists—filled out! She recognized Cal's handwriting.

For a moment she was mortified he'd found her list. What had he thought? Then she began to read it. He had actually jotted brief notes by each of her traits. For a moment she felt disoriented. Dare she consider *Cal* as a possible father for her baby?

He'd meet all the attributes. Even without his notes on the sides she knew that. He was educated and valued it highly—witness the education matching funds he provided employees and the internships he gave promising college students each summer.

He had a wide variety of interests, which made him fit in with every single person he protected, be they heads of states or prominent businessmen.

She knew he had a subscription to the symphony and ballet, as he often gave away tickets when business intruded.

She looked out the window, hearing her sister's voice echo—*you're too involved with Cal.* She wasn't, not in that sense. They worked together—closely. But it was strictly business.

Not that she'd have a problem picturing them kissing. Or doing more.

She banged her head against the glass. She'd never thought of her boss in that way—but only because it would prove too dangerous.

She'd felt a pull of attraction at their first meeting. Getting started in her career had been too important to her to fantasize about a personal relationship. Over the years she'd become used to hearing snippets about his women friends from others. She couldn't compete. And she didn't want to.

She loved her job, relished being considered a colleague, having her opinion sought and listened to. She especially liked the nights when they worked late—sharing dinner, solving impossible scenarios.

She wasn't some empty airhead who thought looks more important than brains. Those were the kind of women he liked to take out.

But there was a hint of pleasure in remembering he'd called her pretty at the cottage.

She folded the paper and stuffed it into her pocket. Grabbing her purse and jacket, she left the office. She was not going to get ideas about her boss. He was so far off-limits she should not even think of him and a baby in the same frame.

Yet every other man she'd seen recently paled in comparison. Was that the problem—Cal set the standard the others failed to meet?

Zoe spent the rest of Sunday wishing she hadn't gone into the office. She'd thrown away the paper and fished it out of the trash twice. Finally she stuffed it in the bottom drawer in her dresser beneath a stack of sweaters. But out of sight did not mean out of mind.

Was he interested?

If so he was too direct not to say something.

At least she believed so.

"Oh, no, what if he did say something?" she exclaimed, horrified and thrilled by the idea.

She started to call her sister, but decided against it. Getting into her car just before dark to head to the beach was her way of coping. She reached the cottage long after nightfall. The sound of the waves soothed her as she turned into the driveway and stopped by the dark house.

If nothing else, the rest of the night would be spent putting Cal out of her mind and trying to figure out a way to find the perfect father for her baby.

Monday morning Zoe arrived at work confident she could handle anything Cal threw her way. She turned on her computer. Ginny came to the doorway.

"Zoe, something's wrong with Cal," she said, looking half frightened.

"What do you mean?" She couldn't imagine anything going wrong for the man.

"I took him the printout he'd requested at the end of work on Friday. Instead of telling me he expected it days ago, he didn't open the door to his office but told me to go away. He's never told me to go away."

"Where's Emily?" Zoe asked of Cal's secretary.

"She wasn't at her desk."

Zoe rose. She'd never heard of such a thing.

"Give me the printout, I'll see he gets it," she said.

In only seconds she was outside Cal's office. Sure enough Emily was not at her desk. What was going on?

She knocked. "Cal, I have the Sanderson's printout."

"Go away," he replied.

She blinked. Opening the door, she stuck her head in, peering around to see him standing by the window, one arm raised and leaning against the casing.

He heard her and turned, glaring at her.

"I don't want to be disturbed."

Instead Zoe stepped inside and closed the door. She crossed to the desk and laid the printout on the messy surface.

"There's definitely something wrong. What is it?"

He frowned at her for a long moment, then the look turned to one of pain. Zoe's eyes widened slightly. She'd never seen Cal like this.

"My uncle died unexpectedly this morning. I just learned of it."

He turned and faced out the window. "We spoke on the phone just a few days ago. Nothing was wrong. At least nothing he told me. The man was only fifty-nine. Too young to die."

Chapter Three

"I'm so sorry," she said, not knowing what to do. The words sounded so inadequate. She was stunned. She never expected anything to throw Jedidiah Callahan a curve. "You two were close?"

"He raised me."

"Oh."

The image of her father rose. She'd be devastated if anything happened to him. Instinctively she went to Cal and leaned against his arm. She couldn't put hers around him; they weren't that close. But she could stand beside him and let him know she was there.

They stood in silence for a long moment, then he sighed.

"I have to go make burial arrangements and see to things. It was just the two of us."

"Where did he live?" she asked.

"Richmond. I grew up there. I visited last August. I talked to him just a couple of days ago. Everything was fine."

She knew he was hurting. And oddly enough she hurt for him.

"I'll go with you," she offered.

"Why?" he said, without moving.

"Because you don't need to be alone at a time like this.

Unless you'd prefer Emily or someone else to go with you? Suzette?"

"Her name is Suzanne and she's the last person in the world to go anywhere with me. Emily has her own family. She's only my secretary."

And I'm only a senior analyst, but I want to go with you, she thought.

"Then I'm it. We'll let Emily know so she can deal with things here. You need to pack and I will, too. Do you want me to drive?"

He wouldn't fit comfortably in her car. But she wasn't sure he should be driving in his current state of mind.

As if she'd said it aloud, he turned and looked at her.

"I'm perfectly capable of driving to Richmond. You'd really go?"

"Yes. I would."

She didn't want anyone to have to deal with loss of family alone.

"You helped me out when I needed it. It's the least I can do for you."

Cal was instantly back in control. He called up department heads and assigned duties. Paged Emily and had her return to the office as soon as she could. Once there, he told her where to find him in Richmond and hustled Zoe out.

"We'll stop at your place first, then mine. It'll take almost two hours to get to Richmond."

She thought it took longer, but then she wasn't used to driving a speed machine.

A quick stop at her apartment for Zoe to pack several outfits, including a black suit that would be suitable for a funeral, and she was back in his car in less than ten minutes.

"Impressive," Cal murmured as he pulled back into traffic.

"What?"

"The speed you're capable of. Most women take longer than that in deciding what lipstick to wear."

"I'm not most women," she said.

The sports car was a dream. She wished Cal would put the top down but it was far too cold. What a great ride it would be in the summer months, though. Would she ever get the chance?

His apartment was not far from her sister's. She was surprised. Though when she thought about it, she couldn't say why, except she always pictured Cal at work, or on an assignment, not lounging around an upscale apartment.

"I'll be equally as fast," he said, pulling into a parking slot beneath the building. "Want to come up?"

"Sure."

He hadn't accompanied her, but she was curious about his apartment.

The elevator whisked them up in seconds. When he opened the door, she was pleased at the warmth of the living space. The muted browns, creams and navy tones went perfectly together. The sofa looked comfortable enough to nap on, and large enough to hold several adults.

"I'll be only a few moments," he said, disappearing down the hall.

Zoe wandered around the living room. The big-screen TV was another surprise. She couldn't picture Cal sitting still long enough to watch a show. He always seemed to have too much energy. There were paintings on the walls—mostly of scenery, though one wall had a grouping of small pictures of New

Orleans scenes. She was charmed by the historic dwellings captured. She wondered what the rest of the flat looked like, but now wasn't the time to ask for a tour.

After all the years she'd known him, she knew so little about him. The years they'd spent together at work didn't give her insight into his life.

In only a couple of moments, he was back and they were on their way.

As they sped south, Zoe wondered what she was doing. She'd worked with Cal, but they weren't precisely friends. Yet she couldn't let him face the coming tasks alone.

"Tell me about your uncle," she said some time later.

She knew talking about people kept their memories alive. Her best friend had died when they'd been in college. She still missed Edie. There weren't too many people around who Zoe could talk to about her friend. Each time helped a bit.

"He never married. Probably thought it would lead to more children and I was enough."

"How did he come to raise you?" she asked.

"He was my mother's brother. When she died, he stepped in. I'm sure he thought my father would eventually return, but he never did."

"Where did he go?"

"Who knows? He took off when I was two weeks old. Couldn't face raising a kid alone after my mom died, I guess. My mother died right after I was born. She had cancer."

"How sad. She missed all of your growing up."

"She should have had treatment, but said it would have harmed the baby. She risked her life to give me mine. The risk didn't pay off. She died at age twenty-two."

Zoe felt a pang of sympathy for the woman she'd never

met. Yet she also felt a connection. She'd risk anything for her baby, including herself.

"I can understand that," she said. "If I can get pregnant, I'll do anything to keep the baby—to give it a healthy life." She glanced at Cal. "You missed knowing her, but she sounds special."

"I heard about her love and sacrifice all my life. My uncle was the one who thought she should have treatment before it was too late. Though he said more than once that there was no guarantee that earlier treatment would have saved her. At least he had me to remind him of her, he often said. It wasn't easy for a single man to raise a kid. Not me, anyway."

She nodded.

"A single parent's role is always hard. That's why God planned for two-parent homes."

"Yet you plan on a single-parent home."

"Maybe. Or maybe I'll find someone I can fall in love with. But either way, I want that father to be around, not to take off like yours did. Did you mean it when you said your uncle was the last of your family?"

"Except me. My mother's parents died when I was small. I never knew my father or his family. I wonder if he even told them I was coming. Anyway, no cousins that I know of. No elderly aunt waiting to dole out comfort and sympathy," Cal said.

"I have lots of family…I can't imagine being alone in the world," she said slowly.

"I'll manage."

She had no doubt, but it still seemed sad.

Sometime later Cal turned off the highway onto a city street. He wound through shopping areas and then residential, ending up pulling into a driveway to an older home. The yard was a bit shaggy, the shrubs overgrown. Despite that, it felt welcoming and inviting. The large front porch was unexpected, and displayed the age of the house. Modern homes rarely had front porches. Thanks to air-conditioning, people didn't sit out much.

"This is it," Cal said, gazing at the home.

Before they could get out of the car, a neighbor came from his house next door and crossed the lawn.

Cal got out to greet him.

Zoe scrambled out and gazed over the car at the two men.

"So sorry," the older man said, reaching out to shake Cal's hand, gripping it with both of his.

"It's a shock. You found him?"

"We were going to the hardware store together. I wanted some hinges, Hal said he needed some paint. JE said you'd be coming home one of these days to give him a hand with the bathroom. So when he didn't answer, I went back and got the key I had and opened the door. He was still in bed. Died in his sleep, it looks like. I'm going to miss him. We've been friends for more than thirty years."

Cal nodded. He glanced at Zoe.

"Sam, I want you to meet Zoe Blackstone, a friend. Zoe, this is Sam Friedman. He was a good friend of my uncle's."

Zoe greeted the man, feeling his sadness at the circumstances. He seemed almost bewildered at the loss of his longtime friend.

Cal spoke with Sam for a little longer, then unloaded the bags from the car. He motioned for Zoe to proceed him to the front door. Putting the suitcases down, he unlocked the door and opened it.

She stepped inside. It was an old home, but clean and kept up.

Cal followed her in and stopped, glancing around.

"It seems strange to know he'll never come from the back of the house when I get home and give me a hug."

"Tell me what I can do," Zoe said.

"See if there's anything for lunch. I'm hungry. Then we can head for the funeral home and do what we've come for."

That night Zoe went to bed in a guest room that looked as if it hadn't been used for a decade. She'd made up the bed with clean sheets. The room was dusted, but not decorated. It was utilitarian, with a few piles of books and other items that looked as if they'd been stashed a while ago and forgotten.

She settled in and stared into the darkness. Cal had managed fine during the afternoon. They'd met with the funeral director and the minister from Hal's church. The service would be in two days.

Cal had gone through the motions appropriately, but she felt the tight control he held. He was grieving yet hiding it behind a wall of strength.

She knew how that felt. She'd cried for weeks when Edie died. She still got sad when she thought about all her friend missed. Zoe had gradually accepted she would forever miss Edie. How much more would Cal miss the man who had raised him?

How much worse would it be if there was no one around to share the grieving with? She was glad she'd come.

The next morning passed in a blur of phone calls, visits from neighbors. Several ladies brought casseroles, for which Cal thanked them profusely. He knew many of the people who stopped by.

Zoe helped where she could, but the majority of the work fell on Cal.

Then there was the somber ride to the church and then the cemetery the next day. Zoe was glad for Cal's sake the turnout for the funeral had been substantial. Hal Larkins had been important in his circle of friends. Many stopped to speak to Cal.

Almost half followed the hearse to the cemetery. The graveside service was brief. Zoe was moved by the minister's words. She glanced at Cal standing at her side. His face could have been carved from stone. She slipped her hand into his and was startled by the sudden grip he gave. He didn't relinquish her hand during the service.

Finally the last words had been said. The last mourners had drifted from the casket. Only Zoe and Cal remained.

"It's time to go," she said softly.

"I know."

She waited a moment, then gave his hand a squeeze and pulled free.

"Say your goodbyes, I'll wait at the car."

The minister stood near the vehicles. He spoke to her as she approached.

"Hal was a fine man. He did his best with his nephew."

"Cal will always miss him, I'm sure," she said.

"Hal was sure proud of him. He often caught me up on some dignitary Cal was guarding. Or some exotic location he visited. It'll seem strange not to have Hal on the left side of the church Sunday mornings. Be sure to remind Cal there will be a meal at the church. The ladies have been working all morning, and many of the mourners will be there. Not quite an Irish wake, but close. We've even rounded up some pictures from Hal's life. Cal figured prominently in lots of them."

"We'll be there," she promised.

It was another ten minutes before Cal walked back to the car.

Zoe reminded him of what the minister had said.

"I hate having to attend. But I will. Uncle Hal would have wanted that. I remember attending those after-funeral meals when I lived with him."

"A way of celebrating a life," she murmured. "His friends will want to talk about him, and give you their condolences."

It was late afternoon by the time Cal turned into the driveway to the old house.

"I'm beat," he said. "I'd much rather devise strategies to foil terrorists than have to do that again. But then, I won't ever have to, will I?"

"Friends will die, there will be other funerals. It's a part of life."

"It sucks."

Zoe nodded.

"After all we ate you probably won't want dinner, but I can make a light snack later, if you like. We'll need something before bed," she said.

He looked at her. His eyes dark and deep.

"Thank you for coming. I did need someone, but didn't realize how much until today. It helped not to be alone."

The rest of the evening was spent separately. Zoe expected he wanted time alone. She roamed the house and found a mystery book in the living room that looked intriguing. Settling in the comfortable sofa, she read away the hours. By the time it was close to her bedtime, she began to get hungry. Rising, she went in search of Cal.

He sat on the stoop at the back door, off the kitchen. It was chilly, but Cal seemed unconcerned with the breeze. The yard was dark, the trees devoid of leaves. Nothing could be seen, except with memory's eye.

She sat beside him.

"You doing okay?" she asked.

Even if he weren't she suspected he wouldn't tell anyone. Had he had a close relationship with his uncle or always been rather independent`?

They sat in silence for a moment, then he spoke.

"Something like this changes one's perspective on life."

"I guess."

"If I'd ever thought about it, I'd have figured him to live to be a hundred. Yet, my mother died young, their parents died before either one reached seventy. I should have thought about that."

"And done what? You said no one suspected he wasn't in robust health. Sometimes these things just happen," Zoe said.

"And they could happen to me, as well."

"Maybe. But you're not your uncle. And half your genes come from another family, maybe one whose members do live to be one hundred. Don't borrow trouble, as my grandmother Elaine always says."

He looked at her in the twilight.

"How is the baby quest going?"

"I haven't found anyone yet, if that's what you're asking."

"But you're still looking, right? I saw the list of attributes you're seeking."

She shrugged.

"I'm trying to match my take of men with what I want. I

noticed you made notes. Interested?" she ended on a joke.

She was embarrassed he knew about her criteria.

"Yes."

Zoe blinked and stared at him. "What?"

"I am interested. Uncle Hal's death changes a lot of things for me. I've been thinking about it all afternoon. I'm the last of my family. When I die, there will be no one to mourn my passing, no one to carry on with knowledge of me in their minds and memories. I want a child, maybe more than one, to be on earth when I'm gone. And I want their mother to be someone I can trust."

"What about one of those women you're always dating?" she asked.

For some reason Zoe had trouble wrapping her mind around the idea of Cal *wanting* to father her baby.

Yet, wasn't that what she was looking for? A man like Cal to be her baby's father? Maybe that was the key—a man *like* Cal, not Cal himself.

"Let me tell you about the last woman I dated. Suzanne Victor was—is—beautiful. She dressed fashionably, could carry a conversation with anyone in Washington and has a beautiful apartment. Her parties are legend. But she's a cold, unfeeling woman who wants nothing more than to be feted and idolized."

"Oh. That's why you stopped seeing her," Zoe guessed, surprised by the cold assessment.

"No, I stopped seeing her because she killed our baby."

Zoe couldn't breathe for a moment. Had she heard him right?

"You two had a baby and she killed it?"

She'd never heard anything like that from Cal.

"She became pregnant and aborted the child because she didn't want stretch marks marring her skin and didn't want morning sickness interrupting her life. I didn't know until the deed had been done. I can never forget. It was pure vanity on her part. A thoughtless, self-centered action that gave no thought to anyone else."

Zoe didn't know what to say. She yearned for a baby so much she couldn't think of anything else. How could a woman abort her own baby for such a frivolous reason? She didn't understand.

"My mother sacrificed her life so I could be born," Cal continued. "You're risking your health holding off that operation to have a baby. I want someone like that to be the mother of my child. Not some vain, selfish, self-centered woman who's more concerned with dresses and parties than the health and well-being of a child. I added to your list on a whim. Or maybe it was fate without knowing what was coming. Not that it matters. Did I pass sufficiently that you'd consider me for your baby's father?"

"This is awkward," Zoe said. "I mean, you know what I want, but somehow I thought I could meet some new man and lead up to it more subtly than this. Are you sure you aren't reacting to the strain and stress of the last few days? The shock of losing your uncle will take a while to get over."

"Getting over the initial shock won't change the facts. I'm thirty-six years old, you know that. If I haven't found someone before this, what are the chances I find someone before I'm too old to be a father?"

"It isn't something you wanted before," she said dryly.

"Because I thought I had all the time in the world."

"So did I. Life's showing me differently. But you can pick and choose."

"I pick you," Cal said.

Zoe blinked. Her heart began to race as she gave full rein to the image of her and Cal trying to make a baby. She clenched her hands into fists and looked away, into the blackness of the backyard.

Could she do this? It was one thing to say she wanted to find a man to make a baby with, something else to actually go through with it. Time was ticking by. There'd be a day soon when she couldn't stand the pain and would have to give in to the inevitable. She'd either do it with a baby or without, but she knew it was coming.

"Let me think about it overnight, if that's okay?" she said at last.

What was there to think about? She couldn't do this. This was Jedidiah Callahan, a man who dated sophisticated women, traveled the world, knew CEOs and senators, for heaven's sake.

And he wanted her to believe he wanted to father her baby?

"Fine." He stood.

She rose beside him.

"Want to order pizza for dinner?" he asked.

And just like that they were back to business colleagues. They'd often ordered in pizza when working late on a project. The shift caught her off guard. She wished she could turn her emotions on and off so easily. She felt she was reeling from his suggestion.

"Yes, pizza's fine."

She'd eat quickly and flee to the safety of the guest room. She'd spend tonight going over his suggestion and then refuse him in the morning.

Cal dialed the pizza place from memory. Many a night he and Uncle Hal had eaten pizza after a ball game, or when both were too tired to fix dinner for some reason or another. Only when he hung up the phone did he wonder if Zoe noticed he'd remembered her choice. Too many late nights working for him to forget what she liked.

She'd gone into the living room while he ordered. He started to follow, but changed his mind. He'd thought about family and babies and life and death all afternoon. Maybe having a baby with Zoe would change his outlook on life. Nothing could change the past.

The future was ahead of him. He'd do his best to be the perfect father for any child he might have. He knew what a good, steadfast father was. He merely had to be like Uncle Hal.

Not the man who had fathered him. He'd never even gone looking for him when he'd become an adult. If the man hadn't wanted him, Cal wanted nothing from him. Not even to meet him.

Would Zoe say yes? It'd make things easier.

He had certain stipulations, however. Would she go for them once he told her?

Used to making quick decisions, he wanted her answer instantly. He didn't want to wait until morning. But he understood her uncertainty. Until he'd told her he wanted to make a baby, she'd been a business colleague. This changed everything.

Maybe she didn't want to sleep with him. He'd never thought about her in that light before, but after considering the situation this afternoon, he knew it wouldn't be a hardship to make love to her.

She was pretty, intelligent, even-tempered. She liked the

work she did, and she did it well. They'd have more in common than most parents did with a common business background and a mutual desire for a baby.

She had to say yes.

Cal awoke early the next morning before the sun was up. He lay in bed for a short while, reviewing all the tasks he needed to do today before heading back to Washington. He planned to take his time in closing up the house.

He'd come down on the weekends for a while, sort through each room and eventually decide whether to sell the place or rent it out. He couldn't see living in it—at least not for a long time. His business was in D.C. But maybe he'd hold on to it and keep it for a retirement place or something. He could always rent it out in the meantime.

He and Uncle Hal had never discussed this scenario. His uncle must have also thought he'd be around for another couple of decades. Wouldn't he have loved to be a grandpa! If he and Zoe did have a baby, he'd always regret his uncle didn't get the chance to see him. Or her. What would it be like to have a little girl? Cal knew nothing about children—but he could learn.

Rising, he quickly showered and dressed in faded jeans and a pullover sweater he'd left in his old room. Walking quietly down the hall, he paused at the guest room. There was no sound. Zoe was still asleep. Had she really considered his suggestion, or was she only waiting until this morning as a stalling technique? It would be awkward if she said no—both for the return trip and work.

It could be awkward if she said yes.

He'd had a night to mull it over himself and still found it a sound idea. She wanted a baby and now so did he. The contrast between Zoe and Suzanne was like day and night. This felt right. He liked her, she liked him. And knowing each other's work habits and schedules would make it even easier to deal with a baby. It was the perfect solution.

If the baby was a boy, would she agree to name him Hal? His uncle would have loved that. Hadn't he urged Cal enough times in the last few years to settle down and start a family? When Cal had countered that Hal had never married, he'd come back with he had his family with Cal—didn't need to have a wife for that.

It was almost nine when Zoe entered the kitchen. Cal had heard the shower earlier and started breakfast. He'd spent the early hours contacting some of his field agents and getting in touch with what was happening in the office. Now it was time to eat. And to talk.

"Good morning," he said when she entered. "The omelets will be ready in a minute. Coffee's on."

"Nice," she said.

He studied her as she poured the hot beverage into a mug. Her hair was glossy brown. He knew it was as soft as it looked from when he brushed it from her cheek at the beach cottage. He'd like to thread his fingers through the tresses and let them drift away. There was faint color in her cheeks—natural not artificial. There was nothing artificial about Zoe.

She looked up and caught him staring, her eyes bright blue. Would any child they made have blue eyes like her or dark like his? Most likely dark. Too bad. She had the prettiest eyes.

"What?" she asked.

"Nothing, I'm hoping you like ham and cheese omelets."

"I do. I also love a man who can cook."

"You've seen the limits of my accomplishments—order pizza and cook omelets. The rest I eat out."

She smiled.

"I like to cook. My mother's a great cook and is used to feeding a crowd. And she made sure every one of us knew how."

They sat at the small table in the kitchen. As soon as Zoe finished the last of her breakfast, Cal nudged aside the plates.

"So, what's it to be?" he asked, impatient to know her answer.

She met his gaze.

"I have a couple of thoughts before saying either way. I don't want to put my job in jeopardy. I love what I do and I'm good at it."

"I don't plan to put your job on the line, either way you decide."

"Well, a relationship like this could become disconcerting to others at the office."

He nodded, not so much in agreement as in encouraging her to get to the point. Yes or no?

She licked her lips. They glistened with the moisture. For a moment Cal stared. He wanted to feel their warmth, kiss away the wetness and taste her sweetness. He swallowed and looked into her eyes again.

She dropped her gaze to her coffee cup, which she was turning around and around. "Actually I hope I made it clear that there's no guarantee I can get pregnant. There's a strong possibility I can, but my doctor said there is also a chance I won't. If you are expecting a sure thing, this isn't it."

"Fine."

He waited, drawing on every ounce of patience he possessed.

She risked another glance up at him. "I suppose we do this scientifically?"

He frowned. "And that is how?"

"I'll know when in my cycle I'm most fertile. I guess we try then."

"And the rest of the time?"

"Go on as normal?" she suggested.

"Meaning?"

"Darn it, you're deliberately making this hard, aren't you?"

A flare of temper surprised him, and gave him insight into how tense she was.

"I'm not trying to. Just lay it out."

"I thought maybe we could go to the sea cottage when it was the right time. Away from our normal places, regular friends and all," she said tentatively.

"Keep it clandestine?"

"Sort of."

"Why?"

"Because if it doesn't work, no one else needs to know," she said quickly.

Cal thought about that a moment. He wasn't sure if he liked the idea or not. What did it matter what other people knew or thought? Then he got it. She was the one who didn't want sympathy if she couldn't conceive. She was guarding herself.

"Okay."

"Okay?" she repeated.

"If that's one of your terms, I'm fine with it. But once you're pregnant, then we tell the world."

She blinked.

"Sure. I'll be thrilled. You can come see him or her whenever you want. That's the whole idea, to have a father who will be there for the baby as he grows up. He'll want to know you and learn from you and all."

"Good point. I have a condition of my own," Cal said.

"You do? Okay. What is it?"

"We get married first."

Chapter Four

"What?"

Zoe hadn't expected anything like that.

"We don't need to get married to have a baby together. I wasn't necessarily looking for a husband, but a father."

"I'm not getting someone pregnant again who has complete control over what happens. If we're married, we both have equal say over the child. Even if we divorce after the baby's born, I'll be the father."

"You'd be the father anyway. I'm not denying the issue. Your name would be on the birth certificate and everything."

"For what it's worth, I think you'll make a terrific mother. And I want to be a part of any child we have from beginning to end. A legal, binding, no-getting-out-of-it connection that everyone in the world will recognize and acknowledge. Think of the baby. Don't you think he or she would like to have both parents around all the time?"

Zoe swallowed; this wasn't what she expected. Her mixed emotions surprised her. She felt a warm glow at his compliment, but was startled by his term. For a few days after her doctor's visit, she'd fantasized about finding someone and falling madly in love in time to have a baby.

She'd known Cal for five years. Yet taking this step

seemed like walking a high-wire without a net. She thought she knew him, but he'd been throwing unexpected curves for the last few weeks.

She secretly wanted a man who'd do anything for her, whether she was cranky or happy. Someone to build a life with, make memories with, to grow old with.

He'd come to the cottage to help her when she was ill. He'd tried to help her by introducing her to Mark. And he came from a strong family tie with his uncle.

She'd never envisioned marriage with Jedidiah Callahan. Could love grow? It hadn't taken much last night to picture them making love. Her idea to escape to the beach cottage was to keep the separate parts of life just that, separate. She didn't want him a fixture at her apartment. How could she have thought she could just tag some man as it and instantly make a baby?

If it was as hard as the doctor suggested to conceive, they'd have to try more than once. If in the end she couldn't conceive, she wanted to come out of any relationship with a whole heart.

"So you're suggesting we marry, have a baby and get divorced—like all within a year?"

"I'm not suggesting anything except if you want me to father your baby, you marry me first."

Suzanne had really done a number on him, she thought.

"You don't love me," Zoe said.

"You don't love me," he replied. "I don't recall you talking about love when you said you would find a man to father your child. Even on that list I made notes on, there was no mention of love. We already know each other pretty well. I'm interested in lots of things. I like sports. I value education. You could count on me being there all his life."

She closed her eyes for a moment. Cal was a good man. She'd been out on several dates over the last couple of weeks with men she hardly knew. None of them had felt right. Time was so short, could she risk the time to meet another three or four men and find none of them appealed to her? There was always the hope that the next man she met would be the love of her life. But what if he weren't? Or the one after? Or the one after that?

Could she take a chance on a man she liked and admired? One she didn't have any trouble picturing kissing her and touching her and making love to her. One who was strong and focused and terrific father material.

Opening her eyes she stared right into his.

"Okay, then. I guess we have a deal."

"I promise I'll do all in my power to keep our child safe and happy," he said.

Zoe gave a half smile.

"So will I. This will be a well-loved child. If I can get pregnant."

For a moment she almost suggested they seal the deal with a kiss.

Instead she stood and carried her dish to the sink. She looked in the cupboard beneath and found soap. Cal also rose and brought his things, putting the dish and cup on the counter next to the sink.

"I'll wash. You cooked breakfast. It won't take long," Zoe said. "I'd like to get going if we're heading back to D.C. soon."

She refused to look at Cal, or even let herself think about the bargain they'd made. She was already having doubts. How could she carry off such a charade? She was so much more comfortable discussing projects or brainstorming security measures than this.

When he moved near, she almost jumped out of her skin. She was aware of Cal as never before. She could see him from the corner of her eye. His shoulders were broad, his posture was quintessential male confidence as he leaned against the counter and watched her.

Soon he'd kiss her. She swallowed, tempted to steal a glance at his mouth. Would that telegraph her curiosity?

She'd bet anything she was going to love his kisses.

Feeling unsettled at the intimacy of her thoughts, she wondered if she should discuss the situation further or hope everything worked out. She knew it would be awkward the first time.

Anticipation and dread began to build. When? Where?

She liked to know ahead of time exactly what was happening. She could see a dozen different scenarios play out, none of them the ideal future she'd once hoped for.

At least she could keep her job, no matter what. She loved her work. If she had waited too long for a family, it would have to be the consolation.

"You analyze things too much," he commented.

"That's what I do, analyze things," she replied, hoping the sudden tension between them would soon dissipate. She couldn't work around Cal if she felt she was walking on eggshells.

"That's your job, but you're carrying it into personal life."

"I do things that way. Always have, which is probably why I'm good at my job. I'm trying to get a handle on how things will play out. Imagine different scenarios, come up with different plans to defuse adverse situations. You know that."

"Probably in ways you can't imagine," he said.

He leaned closer and brushed a few wispy tendrils of her hair from her cheek. Zoe held her breath at the wild feelings that pounded through her at his touch.

"Don't try to foresee the future," he said, watching her hair. "Go with what's happening now. We're two reasonable adults who want a child. We'll have a baby and we'll decide then how we'll proceed. When it's an infant, it'll need you more than me. But once it grows older, we can share the responsibilities and time with him or her."

"I wonder if it'll be a boy or a girl," she said, not wanting to dwell on the actual act of procreating. That would make her crazy.

"Which ever we have, I'm sure we'll both adore the baby."

Too bad the parents didn't adore each other, she thought, though there was sex appeal in spades.

She flicked another glance at Cal and found his dark eyes studying her. Licking her lips quickly, she wondered if he was as attracted to her as she was to him.

Cal leaned back and let his hand drop to his side. He hadn't realized until this moment how much he'd wanted this. And how uncertain he'd been of her answer. Now it was settled. He'd have a baby that no one would ever be able to take away from him. He was more like his uncle and mother than his father. He wanted a child to follow him.

And he'd have a wife. That was nonnegotiable. Maybe not fair to Zoe to saddle her with the condition when he was still trying to protect himself from Suzanne. But he couldn't take that risk another time.

It'd work out. He appreciated her coming with him to deal with this. He knew Zoe had a practical nature that appealed to his own. They'd make this work.

"I'll make the arrangements when we get back," Cal said. "Any special day you'd like to get married?"

"We're not telling anyone, right?" she said.

She could imagine the fuss her mother would make planning a wedding. There'd be friends and neighbors Zoe had known all her life to be invited. All the aunts and uncles and cousins, grandparents. She couldn't see getting away with anything less than a full-blown production that would take months to put together.

A quiet little ceremony would be better. If she didn't get pregnant, she and Cal could quietly get a divorce and no one would be disappointed the marriage hadn't lasted.

Yet she couldn't imagine doing all this without telling Chloe. Her twin could be counted on to keep quiet about it. If she got pregnant, she counted on the excitement her parents would feel about a coming grandchild to counter any hurt at being left out of their daughter's wedding. They had other daughters to plan weddings for.

"Not until you're pregnant," Cal said.

"Then any day suits me," she said.

As soon as the kitchen was clean, they packed up and headed back to Washington. Zoe spent the entire ride worrying about the commitment she'd just made. Was it the best for both of them? Or would they come to regret it?

Cal stopped at her apartment when they reached Washington and insisted on carrying her suitcase up to her front door.

"Do you want to come in?" she asked.

"No, I'm heading for the office. I'll let you know what I arrange."

He nodded once and turned to leave.

Zoe watched him as he strode away. Not even a kiss on the cheek for the future mother of his child. She shivered wondering if she'd done something extremely dumb. Too late now. The bargain was made.

Turning, she entered, putting the suitcase to one side. She then headed for the phone to call her sister.

"Guess what," she said when Chloe answered.

"You found Mr. Right and I'll be an auntie in nine months," Chloe said.

Zoe took a deep breath. What if she did fall in love with Cal? He had all the attributes she wanted in a father. In a husband as well? She shouldn't burden her sister with all the pesky details behind the bargain. Would Chloe try to talk her out of the plan?

"I'm getting married and going to have a baby as soon as we can get me pregnant," she said in a rush.

The silence on the other end lasted several seconds.

"Married? Who's the lucky man?" she asked.

"Cal," Zoe said, then held her breath.

She hears a whoosh of breath across the line.

"I always thought there was something between the two of you. Congratulations. What was it? He got jealous of you seeing all these men and you realized they were dweebs and he was the only man for you?"

Zoe laughed, feeling so comfortable with her sister. Maybe that would be a spin they could give it.

"Something like that. And—he wants a baby as much as I do."

"Well, that's a good thing. Have you told Mom yet? She's going to be thrilled to death."

"No. And don't you tell her, either."

"I won't spoil your surprise. But I'd love to be there when you spring it on her."

"It won't be for a while."

"What won't?" Chloe asked.

"Telling her. Or anyone else for that matter. We want to keep this on the quiet for now."

"Why?"

Good question. It was do or die time. Did she give her sister the real story, or gloss it over? No question, she trusted Chloe.

"It's complicated, but if I don't get pregnant, we'll split."

There was a pause on the other end.

"The jerk. How dare he put such a limitation on your marriage."

"He didn't, I did."

"Are you nuts?"

"Listen, Chloe, I may not be able to get pregnant. You know the doctor said there was a risk I'd never conceive. I don't want to hold a man who wants children to a childless marriage. Would you?"

When she'd mentioned that to Cal, he refused to believe she wouldn't get pregnant. For him it was a non-issue.

"If I loved him to bits and he loved me, children would be a bonus, not the main focus of the relationship," Chloe said slowly.

"Still, it is my decision and I don't want others knowing yet."

"What does Cal say about that?" Chloe asked.

"He thinks we will get pregnant."

"Good for him—he's an optimist. I like the way he thinks.

So are you moving into his place or he into yours? When are you getting married? What are you going to tell Mom and Dad when you do get pregnant? Oops, guess we forgot to tell you about our wedding?"

"That's something we'll have to deal with when and if the time comes. Maybe we could have a ceremony for the family then."

"I'm coming over. I want to see you face-to-face to make sure about this," Chloe said.

Zoe sighed. She loved her sister, but sometimes she was too astute.

"I'll be home all day. Come when you can."

Might as well give in to the inevitable. Chloe was a force to be reckoned with.

Cal called Zoe after nine that evening. She'd showered and prepared for bed, curled up in a favorite chair in her pajamas reading a good book when the phone rang.

"I made arrangements for next Tuesday. I had Emily check your schedule for that day. No appointments noted on your calendar. Does that work for you?"

"Tuesday it is."

She felt a zing of anticipation. After the wedding, would he want to sweep her away somewhere and get started on that baby? Or would he honor their agreement and wait for her to tell him when she was most fertile?

She wished she had her calendar handy—maybe the two dates collided. Or maybe she should forget that restriction. Being more proactive could be a good thing.

"We'll go to the courthouse in Arlington. No waiting for a license in Virginia. A local judge will marry us."

"Fine." It was a good thing she never pined for a white

dress and a dozen bridesmaids. It was never going to happen.

"Did you want a honeymoon?" he asked.

Zoe was startled by that thought.

"I didn't expect one. But we can drive over to the beach, if you like, spend the night at the cottage."

It'd be something out of the ordinary for a wedding night, even if not super special.

"What did you do today after you got home?" Cal asked.

"I told my sister about us. Chloe came right over and gave me the third degree. But she's cool with keeping it quiet. She's not quite as optimistic as you that I'll conceive."

Zoe wasn't going to tell him how Chloe was convinced that Cal would never want a divorce no matter the outcome with a baby. But then, her twin still thought there was a closer tie to this relationship than there was.

Zoe couldn't tell her it was totally a business arrangement—not in light of her sister's happy marriage.

"How were things in the office?"

"Hectic as usual. But I cleared my calendar for Tuesday and can rearrange a couple of appointments Wednesday morning."

He began to talk about an upcoming visit of an important businessman from Brazil, and Zoe shifted gears into business mode. Chloe would be horrified to find a newly engaged couple preferred to talk business than about themselves, but Zoe felt closer to Cal discussing business than their marriage.

Once the conversation ended, Zoe called her mother to make sure no one had plans for the sea cottage. October was not a month most of the family liked to visit the beach. She loved walking along the windy coast and watching the breakers. But next week she didn't want anyone to arrive unexpectedly. No one planned to use it that her mother knew about.

"You're taking some time off, honey?" her mom asked.

"Might go there for a couple of days. I love it in the fall."

"I prefer it warm and sunny."

"It'll probably be sunny," Zoe said, knowing her mother loved sitting on the warm sand beneath a wide umbrella and reading.

She rarely went into the water or into the sun, but enjoyed being lazy and watching others take advantage of the water.

"But not warm. Bundle up well."

Zoe agreed, smiling. No matter how old she was, her mother was still Mom.

Despite the fact it wasn't a love match, or even an auspicious night as her calendar reminded her when she checked, Zoe wanted something nice to be married in and something sexy to wear that first night.

She was having second thoughts, and third and fourths as well. During the day, she tried to ignore the upcoming nuptials and treat Cal like she'd always done. But during one staff meeting, her mind wandered to what it would be like to be married to him. He was a dynamo around the office, expecting the most from those who worked for him. He knew his business and made sure everyone was on the same wavelength for various projects. He was tough but fair. And unswerving in his goals.

Of course he was also the best looking male in the office, in her opinion. Could she really be married to him?

At night she dreamed of a future with a small baby crying for cuddling, Cal hanging over her shoulder as she nursed their child. It was the getting-to-that-point that she glossed over.

But anticipation built, alternating with delight and dread. One night before too long she and Cal would make love.

That thought scared her to death.

Late Tuesday afternoon Mr. and Mrs. Jedidiah Callahan headed east to the beach. The ceremony had been brief, and rather perfunctory, Zoe mused as Cal's car sped along. The judge who married them had read the words from a book and seemed bored by the process. The witnesses were his secretary and law clerk. No one from Zoe's family was there. Cal had no one to attend.

Zoe glanced at her left hand. The plain gold band Cal had placed there gleamed in the sunshine. Because the marriage was to be secret she hadn't thought about rings. She wouldn't wear it after today. Not in the office, not at home. She clenched her hand into a fist as if to hold on tight. For today, however, anyone they met could know they were married. Her heart warmed slightly at the sight of the gold band.

"Do we need to stop for groceries?" he asked after a long silent spell.

"Unless you want to eat out every meal. There are only canned and packaged goods at the cottage. We never know if the power has gone out, so don't keep perishables unless someone's in residence. I cleared out the fridge when I left last time," Zoe said. "Practically speaking, it'd be better to eat in. Going to the local restaurants could give rise to gossip that would get back to my family."

"Tell me the best place to stop," he replied with a quick, enigmatic look at her.

"Steubensville would be a good place. It's not too far from Seagrass Point that cold foods would get warm, but not so close we'd likely run into anyone who knows me. My family has been staying off and on at Seagrass Point since my grandfather was a kid."

Being in a clandestine marriage would take some getting used to. Zoe wasn't used to subterfuge. Every time she had an attack of conscience, she remembered the possibility of not being able to have a baby. She wasn't sure she could stand the well-meaning sympathy of others if that turned out to be the situation. Better to protect herself from future pity.

The cottage was cold when they entered. Zoe quickly fired up the wall heater while Cal brought in their bags and the sacks of groceries.

"It's only four o'clock. Too early to start dinner. Why don't we change and take a walk along the beach," she suggested.

Even though the house was huge by most standards, she felt it shrink with Cal in the room. She'd pointed out one of her brothers' rooms as a place Cal could use for the night.

"Good idea. You can tell me all about growing up spending summers here," he said.

The beach had held Zoe's heart since she'd been a little girl. She'd always loved the timelessness of the breakers, the soothing calmness being here brought.

Today her nerves were stretched tight. She was counting on the ocean to work its magic to help her relax.

Cal looked more masculine than ever when he joined her a short time later. She'd put on warm jeans and a sweatshirt. Her jacket was lightweight but should help if it was windy.

He'd donned dark pants and a black sweater, which defined his wide shoulders and broad chest to perfection and made him look slightly mysterious. Zoe realized she didn't know this man she'd married as well as she thought. Maybe in business, but his personal life was a complete unknown. She felt her heart kick up another notch. It was going to be a long evening.

"Did you ever go to the beach as a child?" she asked when they headed out.

"Uncle Hal took us for a week every couple of years when I was younger. We went to Virginia Beach. Always in the summertime and it was always crowded. This is different. We're the only people on the beach."

"It's crowded here in the summer months, but only the year-round people in town use the beach this time of year. And a few crazies like me. I think I prefer winter to summer. Though I do like to swim."

"Ever do any sailing?"

"From time to time. One of my brothers loves it. He has a boat he keeps up at Annapolis. We all go out on it at least once each season. I think he'd live on it if he could. Do you sail?"

"I have. I like it, but owning a boat is a big commitment and so is Protective, Inc. That's where my focus lies at the moment."

"How did you get into this business, I mean actually start up a company that provides protection to high-profile people?" she asked.

"Saw the need and stepped in. I had training in the Rangers, which prepared me for strategic planning of protective measures. The rest is learning as we go, seeing what works, what can be improved, tapping into the brains of the people who work with me. Keeping abreast of new technologies."

"What do you see changing if you become a father?" she asked.

"When I become a father. Spending more time at home. Learning how to take care of a child." He glanced at her again. "I'll be there for the kid."

She tried to imagine him holding an infant, but she could more readily picture him fighting terrorists.

When they returned to the cottage, it was time to begin preparing dinner. Zoe was glad of the task as it kept her from dwelling on this odd arrangement. She'd known and admired Cal for a long time, yet felt awkward and uncertain around him with the changed circumstances.

"Need help?" he asked, walking into the spacious kitchen.

"Since we planned on spaghetti, you have your choice of fixing the garlic bread, the salad or pasta. I'm good on the sauce."

"I'll start on the bread," he said.

A few moments later they were companionably working side by side at the counter.

"I thought your cooking was limited to omelets and ordering pizza," she said, watching him expertly slice the bread and smear it with a garlic-butter spread they'd purchased.

"This is hardly gourmet cooking. Uncle Hal made sure I knew how to do things, I choose not to. This is different. Any idiot can prepare garlic bread."

"My brother Sean can't." She thought about it for a moment. "Or maybe he just pretends he can't to get out of helping. I wouldn't put it past him."

"Sean, older or younger?"

"He's older by two years, and another one of twins. Declan is his. You'd think my mother would have caught on after they were born, but nope, she then had me and Chloe."

"Four kids, a houseful," he said.

Zoe laughed softly. "Actually I have ten brothers and sisters, there are eleven of us."

"Good grief."

Cal stopped work to stare at her.

"Unexpected in an only child raised by an uncle, I expect," she said with a smile. "Actually it does shock most people in this day and age. Large families aren't in vogue anymore. But Mom and Dad love us all and I can't imagine not having so many brothers and sisters around."

"No wonder this place is so large," he said glancing around.

"It still gets crowded in summer."

"Had things been different, did you want a large family?" Cal asked, wrapping the bread in aluminum foil and turning to check if the oven had been turned on.

"I knew I always wanted children, but to me, getting my career underway was paramount. Then I thought I'd marry and have kids. But that was vague and general. Now it looks as if I'll be lucky to have even one."

"Maybe you'll have twins."

"Maybe. Start the water for the pasta, would you?"

As preparations continued, Zoe began to grow more at ease.

Cal hunted in the cupboard where the pans were coming up with a deep one. While he filled it, Zoe asked, "So did you want a large family?"

"I never thought about it. One day I figured I'd get married and have the average 2.5 children. Uncle Hal was forever after me to get started, he had a fear I'd end up like him—a bachelor all his life."

"Today changed that," she murmured.

It seemed surreal. She was a married woman and still felt as uncertain as any employee entertaining the boss. She studied the glint of gold on her finger for a moment.

Zoe set their places on a small table in the living room feeling it would be more intimate than the large kitchen table. If things went well, she'd like to have a nice memory of her wedding night.

Talk inevitably turned to work. They discussed upcoming visits by various dignitaries and businessmen they had been hired to help. Strategies to keep them from the public eye, how to let them do all they wanted in Washington without putting any in jeopardy with fanatical groups. And the recent request to accompany a Congressional member's family when they toured a Middle East country.

They talked long past ten. When Zoe realized the time, she jumped up.

"I'll do these dishes and let you get to bed."

Cal leaned back lazily and watched her.

"Efficient as ever. But I rarely go to bed this early. Do you?"

Zoe nodded.

"I get up really early to run, so I usually go to bed around ten."

"I'm a runner," he said. "I imagine the beach is great for that."

"If I don't get out almost before dawn in the summer, it's too hot. But the packed sand is the best surface to run on and I love it this time of year. Join me tomorrow?"

"Yes."

He rose and carried the rest of the items from the table to the kitchen.

When Zoe bid him good-night a few moments later, she didn't know if she should offer a kiss on the cheek or not. She'd have to touch him sometime. Before many more days passed they'd be doing a lot more than touching.

"Wake me if I'm not up when you are ready to run," Cal said, taking the decision from her.

Sometime later, Zoe lay in bed, the pretty nightgown she'd bought still folded in her suitcase. She'd donned her comfy sweats, warm enough for the old house in winter. Not exactly a fashion statement, she thought as she drifted to sleep. She bet Suzanne never wore sweats a day in her life.

Zoe awoke suddenly. She looked into the darkness, wondering why she was awake. Peering at the clock, she saw it was only a bit after midnight. She hadn't slept for long. Straining to hear anything unusual, she only heard the soft rhythm of the sea kissing the shore.

Turning, she caught a glimmer of light. Was Cal up?

Throwing back the comforter, she rose and found socks to put on her feet. Softly she padded into the living room. Cal sat on the sofa his laptop open on his legs. He looked up when she entered.

"Did I wake you?" he asked.

"I don't think so. What are you doing? Have you been to bed?"

"Not yet. Just catching up on reports. This is the best time to do that—no interruptions."

"Mmm." She sat beside him on the sofa and looked at the screen. "Agent reports?"

"Yes. This is Steve Carrington's assessment. It'll be on your desk when we get back for further analysis."

She leaned a bit closer, reading the terse words.

"He sounds worried…not like Steve. Do you think it'll become critical?"

Zoe could feel Cal's warmth. She tried to focus on the report, but her hormones must be acting up. She noticed Cal wore the same dark pants he'd had on earlier. But he'd taken off his shoes and socks. She wondered if his feet were cold. They were large, and sexy.

She blinked and stared at the screen, not seeing a thing. Sexy feet? She had five brothers whose feet she'd seen all her life. Feet weren't sexy.

Except on Cal.

Was she losing her mind?

He pointed to a line on the screen and his arm brushed against her. She almost caught her breath at the sudden spark of excitement that hit. What would it be like if he put his arm around her shoulder and pulled her close. Turned her face for a kiss.

The light was dim in the living room, the brightest point the laptop screen which provided plenty of illumination to see him clearly. Including the faint lines radiating from his eyes, the day's growth of beard on his jaw.

He turned to look at her.

"What do you think?"

Yes, was all she wanted to say. But he was talking about a report, not how she was thinking.

"It would take some analysis, but I think his instincts can be counted on."

"I agree. I want you to get on it first thing."

"Sure."

She swallowed and looked back at the laptop. The words *I want you* echoed. She almost missed the second part of the sentence. She was going crazy.

The chirping of Cal's cell sounded loud in the silent night. He reached out to the table and picked it up.

"Callahan," he said.

Zoe watched his expression. He gave so little away, but she noted the slight tightening around his eyes and the way his jaw clenched.

"Calm down," he said.

She wondered who was calling so late and what was going on that he had to try to calm the caller.

"Where's Peterson?"

Jim Peterson and Shelley Harris were on assignment together shepherding around some college-aged daughters of a United Nations diplomat who was visiting Washington. Shelley was new, but she got the assignment as the only female agent available. Something had obviously happened to have her calling Cal in the middle of the night.

"I'm not home. It'll take me a couple of hours to get there. I'll head out now. Get Peterson and find those girls."

He clicked off the phone and powered down the laptop as he explained to Zoe, "Shelley's assignments ditched her. They have been hitting bars and clubs all night, and every time things got out of line, Shelley or Jim stepped in, to the dismay of those spoiled young women. Finally they claimed they had to use the ladies' and never returned. Jim's contacting cab companies and Uber to see if anyone picked them up at that club. Shelley has searched high and low throughout the club and local neighborhood and can't find them. I have to get back to Washington."

"I'll be ready in a second. I can wear these if you'll drop me at home once we get back."

Quickly packing, and getting the perishables from the refrigerator and putting them in a bag with ice, Zoe was ready to depart in less than five minutes. Cal had been ready in three.

He maneuvered through the empty streets of Seagrass Point in no time and soon had them speeding on the highway for Washington.

Slowly Zoe eased the ring from her finger and held it in her palm for a moment. Opening her purse, she slipped it into her change compartment. They were in full work mode, no time for might-have-beens.

She was not disappointed. Well, only a little.

It was after three when they reached Zoe's apartment building. Cal insisted on going up with her. He waited until she opened the door, then put her bag and the food just inside.

"I'll take a rain check on that run," he said.

She nodded. "Go, they need you."

"It wasn't the wedding day I know you expected. If you get pregnant, we can do it over with all your family."

"It's fine."

"No, it's not." He pulled her into his arms and kissed her.

Chapter Five

It was unexpected. It was glorious. It was as if she had never been kissed before. Her toes curled, her knees threatened to give way. His arms held her pressed against him. She could feel every muscle in that solid chest. But her mind could accept little beyond the pure pleasure of his mouth, his lips moving against hers, his tongue pressing her lips.

When he deepened the kiss, she knew she wanted it more than anything she'd ever craved before. Locking her arms around his neck, she held on, giving back as good as she got, feeling the flare of awareness that threatened to burst out of control. If they stayed this way forever it would end too soon for her.

But end it did, when Cal reluctantly pulled her arms down, sliding his hands down to grip hers.

"I've got to go."

She nodded, wishing he'd done this when they first reached the cottage. How differently the night might have turned out.

Raising her gaze to his, she found her voice.

"I know. Go find those girls and charge the parents extra for not raising them right."

Amusement lit his eyes. "That's one tactic I've not tried.

Does it work?"

She shrugged, her hands clinging to his. Forcing herself to release his grip, she pulled back.

"I'll be at work on time."

"Good."

He leaned in and brushed his lips against hers lightly, then turned and hurried off.

"Good grief," Zoe said as she closed the door, leaned against it and slowly slid down until she was sitting on the floor. She felt more alive than at any time in her life. She could move mountains.

She wanted to call her sister and ask if this was the feeling she had when her husband kissed her. She suspected it was.

Oh, wow, when could they do it again?

Maybe there's be more to this marriage gig than she expected.

Only—she had to watch things. To Cal she was a means to an end. As he was for her.

The kiss changed all that. Now she wanted more. Wanted to learn every single thing about the man. Was it too late to change the parameters of their agreement? Tell the world, live together and pray a baby came before it was too late?

Spying the bag of groceries, starting to look damp with melting ice, Zoe scrambled up and took the food to the kitchen. Practicality was called for, not daydreams. She had to be at work early. She'd better get some sleep.

Having been up most of the night, she thought she'd fall asleep as soon as her head touched the pillow, but not so. Instead she relived every heart-stopping second of that kiss. Savoring every remembered touch, feeling, delight.

Zoe found it more difficult than she'd expected to walk

into work the next morning as if nothing had changed in her life—or rocked her world. She checked with Emily to see if Cal was in, but he wasn't. Emily reported there'd been a crisis in the night and he was in the field. Zoe didn't reveal she knew the situation, merely asked if she could have some time with him when he returned to the office.

It was difficult to get back into the swing of the routine, but by midmorning, the memory of the kiss had been pushed aside as she updated her information on the situation in Eastern Europe that looked like it was about to explode.

Twice she called Steve Carrington, but couldn't reach him. Had things gone from bad to worse in the meantime?

By lunch she had found the source of the problem and had finally talked to Steve. It looked as if the situation was becoming less volatile. How had the others fared with the missing girls from last night?

When Zoe returned from lunch, there was a message from her doctor's office. She called and the nurse asked her to wait as the doctor wanted to speak to Zoe.

"How are you feeling?" the doctor asked when she got on the line.

"Fine right now."

"There is an opening on the operating schedule in a couple of weeks, I could slot you in."

"I'm going to try for a baby," Zoe said firmly.

There was a pause on the other end of the line.

"You may not be able to become pregnant," the doctor said.

"I know, but I need to try. If it doesn't work, I'll know I did all I could. If it does, then I'll get to have a child before the operation removes that possibility forever."

"If I were your age, I'd do the same thing," the doctor said. "Let me know if you need stronger medication for the cramps. And come see me the minute you think you have conceived. Good luck."

Heartened by the doctor's words, Zoe felt better than she had since she'd heard the prognosis.

She eyed her calendar. It would be another two weeks before she would be most fertile. For a moment she regretted the delay. After that mind-blowing kiss last night, she couldn't wait to make a baby with Cal.

It was late afternoon when Cal asked Emily to call Zoe and ask her to join him. His day had gone from bad to worse and this was the first moment he had to catch up. When he heard Zoe by Emily's desk, he went to the door in time to catch his secretary warning her to be quick.

"He's running behind everywhere because of taking time off yesterday and the crisis last night. So don't take any longer than you need."

Zoe nodded and met Cal's eyes as she stepped into his office.

He shut the door and swept her into an embrace, files and all. He had thought all day about that kiss and had been counting the minutes until he could kiss her again. She gave a soft squeak of surprise and then met his every move. The files impeded her own embrace, but he didn't care. Her mouth was what he craved and she was as hot and sweet as he remembered.

Finally he pulled back, gazing down at her. She gave him a sassy look.

"So that's what being married to the boss is like," she said.

"Sometimes. What is all that?"

"Carrington's files."

He ran his fingers through his hair and stepped away.

"Not to worry, the situation's been resolved. There was a slight glitch in our initial estimates of the strength of the terrorists . He's been apprised and has already found a way to circumvent the stronghold. I'd say the man he's guarding will continue to be safe."

She laid the complete report on his desk.

"Thanks. I knew I could depend on you."

"Did you find the missing girls?"

"Yes, at a club they'd already visited. Some young men there lured them back. I think we successfully put the fear of God into them, and made sure their parents knew we don't deal with people who don't fully cooperate with the agency."

"So no surcharge for bad parenting?" she said whimsically, her eyes on his lips.

It was all Cal could do to walk around his desk and glance at the folder. If she looked at him like that for much longer he'd say forget any agreement and take her to bed tonight.

"The girls appeared suitably chastised and promised not to do such a thing again. I think Shelley wanted to smack them, but she refrained," he said, not looking at Zoe again.

He needed a minute to get control.

Zoe laughed.

"Good. Well, I won't stay any longer. I wanted to put your mind at rest over the Carrington situation."

"You busy tonight?" he asked, looking up then.

She blinked. "No."

"Have dinner with me."

"Dinner?"

"Is that so odd for a married couple to eat together?"

"Not for a real married couple."

"Make no mistake, our marriage is real."

"Okay, maybe I meant, conventional married couple. Never mind, I'd be glad to have dinner with you. Where shall I meet you?"

"I'll pick you up around six-thirty. I need to get home and shower first."

"You're in the same clothes you had on when we left the sea cottage. Haven't you been home yet?"

He shook his head.

"You must be tired. Let's not go out. I can fix something at my place and then you can go home. Or better yet, how about I bring food to your place and then when we finish eating, you can go right to bed?"

Cal laughed aloud.

"You'll make the perfect mother. I'm fine, Zoe. A little tired, maybe, but not on my last legs. I'll take you up on the offer of a home-cooked meal. But I'll come to your place so you don't have to drive yourself home later. Thanks for the concern."

Cal arrived at Zoe's shortly before seven. He'd gone home to shower and change as he'd said and felt more alert. Time was when he could stay up two or three nights without many effects. Apparently those days were gone.

Zoe greeted him and offered him a glass of wine.

"Dinner will be ready soon," she said. I only have to quickly steam the veggie."

"Need help?" he asked, following her into the kitchen, glancing around and taking in the touches of color and knickknacks she displayed.

It reminded him a bit of Uncle Hal's place in that it was

restful and relaxing.

"Not at all. Go sit down, you look tired."

So much for feeling his shower rejuvenated him. He prowled the small living room, stopping at her bookshelf to read the titles of some of her books. She liked mysteries and romance novels. Wandering to the window, he looked at the nondescript view. Nothing like the one from his flat.

He was turning to sit on the sofa when she called, "It's ready," a few minutes later, and entered carrying already served plates to the small table in one corner that served as her dining area. It had been set with silverware earlier and Cal watched as Zoe carefully centered the dishes at each place.

"I'll get the wine and we'll be ready," she said, making a quick trip back to the kitchen.

"How long have you had this apartment?" he asked sometime later.

Their plates were almost empty. He'd filled her glass, and his, once more. The woman was a good cook. He hoped she offered more home-cooked meals.

"Since I started working for you. The salary I received enabled me to get a bigger place than I had before. I like the location and my neighbors."

"What you earn now could get you an even bigger home."

She shrugged.

"This suits me. I'm saving my money. Who knows, I might need it if I have a baby."

"Why?"

"Maybe I'll take a leave of absence from my job to stay home the first year. I'd need something to replace my income."

"I'd support you if you choose to do that," he said.

He lifted his glass and studied the wine for a moment. "This is good."

She nodded, watching him thoughtfully.

"I didn't agree to marriage with the expectation you'd end up supporting me."

He shrugged. It was only money.

"We'll decide together what's best for the baby. Tell me more about your family."

"What do you want to know?"

"What was it like growing up a twin?"

Zoe looked pensive for a moment.

"I never knew any difference. Chloe and I have always been close. We did things together the two of us all the time and yet were always a part of the family. With so many kids, my folks were hard-pressed to give each of us individual time, but they did. Would you like twins?"

"It would be a good solution to having more than one child if you only have one shot at pregnancy," he said.

The reality of his marrying her for a child rose. For a moment he wondered if she'd glow like some pregnant women did. He'd see all the changes in her body, in her attitude. Rejoice when the baby was born. Have a link to the future. Suddenly Cal wanted Zoe to have his baby more than anything.

Could they do it? Make a baby together? What were the odds she'd deliver twins? They ran in her family, but he'd heard twins skipped generations. Maybe they'd end up with twin grandchildren.

Grandchildren.

He stared at Zoe. Would they still be married then? Would they learn to deal with each other and find an affection or genuine liking that went beyond what they had now?

She was looking at him with questions in her eyes. Cal drew a breath and looked away.

"Dinner was delicious. Thank you for cooking instead of choosing a restaurant," he said easily.

"Do you think about the future?" she asked, suddenly wondering if he was as confused by the way things were going as she was.

"I plan the best I can."

"I don't mean work. What if we have a baby. He or she will grow up, and one day we'll be grandparents. Did you ever think of that?"

Amusement showed in his dark eyes. Did she read minds?

"The thought crossed my mind."

"So, what if it happens?"

"Then I expect we'll deal with it."

"I want close family ties, laughter and sharing at holidays, rallying around when someone needs something. Memories and fun times and bedrock loyalty."

Cal would give a lot to be included in that.

"Never mind. We aren't even expecting a baby yet and I have us as grandparents already. Go sit on the sofa. I'll bring coffee and dessert," she said, breaking out of her musings.

"All this and dessert, too?" Cal asked.

"Chocolate cake."

"My favorite."

He couldn't remember the last time someone had made a cake for him.

Zoe quickly did the dishes while the coffee was brewing. His slow smile when she'd mentioned the cake had her stomach turning somersaults. Once the hot beverage finished brewing, she prepared their cups and plates with generous slices of cake. Carefully carrying them into the living room on a tray, she stopped when she saw Cal lying on the sofa, fast asleep.

She quietly placed the tray on the coffee table and sat on the nearby chair.

"Cal?" she said softly.

There was no response.

Sighing, Zoe picked up her plate and began to eat, watching her husband of two days sleep. Sipping her coffee a few moments later she wondered if she should wake him up to go home, or leave him to get the first sleep he'd probably had in more than forty-eight hours. She opted for letting him sleep. She picked up the tray and took everything back to the kitchen. Putting the cups in the sink and wrapping his piece of cake to keep it fresh, she turned off the light and headed for her room. She had a warm afghan she'd cover him with. She hoped he wouldn't get cold during the night.

Zoe had no trouble falling asleep. Cal had to be exhausted. He hadn't slept at all last night. She hoped he was comfortable enough on the sofa.

Zoe had just come from the bathroom the next morning when she heard the knock on her front door. Running to get it before the sound woke Cal, she skidded to a stop when she reached the living room just as he opened the door to Chloe.

"Oh," her twin said. "I didn't wake you two, did I?"

"Not at all," Cal said and opened the door wide.

"Hi, Chloe. What brings you here so early?" Zoe asked, walking over to her sister and giving her a kiss on the cheek.

She looked warily at Cal. He didn't know how she'd presented this to her sister.

Cal closed the door and leaned against it, looking from one to the other. He let his gaze briefly track down the length of the robe Zoe had donned, but his interest appeared to be more in the similarities of the two women.

"I have a breakfast meeting and swung by to see how things were going. Well, I take it…" Chloe said, flicking a look at Cal. Her smile was sunny.

"Perfect," he said, pushing away from the door and crossing to stand beside Zoe.

She almost jumped when his hand came up to her nape and gently massaged.

"We haven't had breakfast yet. Would you care to join us for coffee or something?" he asked.

Zoe wanted to double-check the tie of the robe, to make sure the opening was secured. She felt distinctively at a disadvantage as the only one not dressed in the group.

And his actions were inexplicable. He knew Chloe understood this wasn't a real marriage unless there was a baby. What was he doing touching her neck until she was shivering with a tingling awareness that thrust out every cohesive thought?

"Coffee would be lovely," Chloe said, turning to put her purse down on one of the tables.

"I'll get it started while you go get dressed," he said to Zoe, leaning over to kiss her briefly.

She stayed in one spot as he easily crossed to the kitchen. Would he know where to find anything? Glancing at her sister's speculative look, she smiled brightly and dashed back to the bedroom. Things were spinning out of control. What if it had been her parents who had showed up unannounced? Not that they ever had—but they could.

And what was Cal doing? The caress, the kiss. If she dared spend a second apart from the other two, she would sit on her bed and try to figure things out. But with him in that kind of mood, and her sister arriving unexpectedly, which was totally out of character, she dared not leave them alone for longer than it took to dress.

In record time, she returned to the living room. Cal sat at the small table with Chloe, both had a wary look about them. What were they discussing?

"Coffee ready?" Zoe asked, looking at one then the other.

"Should be. One great trait of your sister is her speed in dressing and packing," Cal said to Chloe.

"She has other great traits," her twin returned.

"I know."

"Hello, you two, I'm right here. Chloe, if you're going to be snippy, you can leave," Zoe said, growing annoyed.

"I'm cranky, ignore me. I'd much rather be sleeping in."

Zoe nodded, gave Cal a speaking look and continued to the kitchen for the coffee.

"So what's up with your sister?" Cal asked after Chloe had left twenty minutes later.

"I'm not sure."

"She's obviously protective toward you. Does she think I'm going to do something to harm you?"

Zoe shook her head. "She thinks you're going to bail if we don't conceive and she resents that on my behalf," Zoe said without looking at him.

She gathered the empty cups to give herself something to do.

"Why would she think such a thing?" he asked.

Zoe licked her lips and tried to think up an excuse that

would fly without coming out with a lie.

"Just say it," he said.

"She thinks there's more to this marriage than there is," she blurted out, balancing the cups and saucers. Slowly she walked into the kitchen.

Cal pushed back his chair and followed her.

"Such as?" he asked from the doorway.

"Genuine caring between us."

He studied her for a moment.

"I'd agree with that, wouldn't you?"

"Maybe," she said slowly. "I told her we were more involved than she suspected. I couldn't tell her the entire truth. She'd worry too much."

He stared at her for a moment, his expression closed. Then he gave an abrupt nod and turned back to the living room.

"Want to grab breakfast on the way into work?"

She blinked at the lack of follow-up. Was that it? He was letting it go? No comment, no suggestion that she clear the air?

"Aren't you going home to change first?" she asked, stalling.

The sooner she got alone, the better.

"I plan to but we can stop for a meal first."

"I'll get a bagel at the coffee shop next to the office. I have lots to do today."

What Zoe really wanted to do was get some time to herself. She was growing more stressed the longer she was around Cal. It seemed easy for him to portray a role. The brief kiss he'd given her had been for Chloe's benefit. But Zoe couldn't turn her emotions on and off so easily.

"I apologize for falling asleep last night," he said. "It wasn't my intent when I arrived."

"You were exhausted. It wasn't a problem."

Did he look embarrassed? She couldn't imagine anything disconcerting Cal.

"Except I missed cake."

She smiled. "Want a piece now?"

"Yes."

Watching while he ate the cake, Zoe should have been delighted at the carefree glimpse she was getting of a man she thought was totally business oriented. Instead, she felt as if she were sitting on an edge of a cliff and could topple over with the slightest push.

When Cal stood by the table, he looked at her.

"What we need is a honeymoon," he said.

"What?"

It was the last thing in the world she expected. And the last thing they needed. Was he crazy?

"We don't know each other beyond work. If we're to present a convincing front to your family and friends when we go public, I think we need to find out more about each other. I would never send in an agent if he or she hadn't been briefed. I don't feel briefed."

It made sense. But the images that flared had nothing to do with sharing information. Honeymoons were more physical—like sharing a room and a bed, kisses. Her imagination went into overdrive.

"Write me up a bio," she said, stalling, hoping he couldn't guess her thoughts.

He shook his head.

"Too brief. We'll spend a couple of days together this weekend. That'll give us a good start."

"I don't know," she said, hoping inspiration would come fast so she could get out of spending more time with Cal. Until she needed to.

It wasn't as if she didn't like being with him, but he made her nervous, self-conscious. Ever since that kiss.

"Consider it prepping for an assignment," he said.

"I'm an analyst—I don't go out on assignment."

"Yet you've taken this one. And maybe we need to get the hurdle of the first time out of the way."

Thursday flew by. Friday afternoon Cal called Zoe in her office. She'd seen him in passing at work. She half expected him to offer lunch or dinner, but according to Emily when Zoe asked about his schedule, Cal was inundated with meetings and small crises that required his attention.

When he called Friday, Zoe picked up, surprised to hear him if he was that busy.

"I'll pick you up around six. Do you want to eat around in town or wait until we're on the road?" he asked.

"You still want to go?"

They had decided to try the cottage again.

"Oh, yes, I most definitely want to go away with you," he said very deliberately.

She rubbed her forehead, trying to think.

"Fine. I'll be ready at six. And I'd like to eat at Katie's Steak House. It's about half way between here and Seagrass Point."

"Sounds good. See you then."

He hung up without another word.

By the time six o'clock arrived, Zoe had changed clothes twice and made a mess of her bedroom choosing and discarding clothes to take to the cottage. Each member of the family had a dresser at the cottage with assorted beach clothes to save packing and unpacking for short stays.

None of those outfits were quite what she wanted to wear around Cal. She refused to examine why this was important to her, but it was.

She left the apartment a few moments before six and arrived at the lobby door just as Cal pulled up. Before he could park, she waved and hurried to the car. He stowed her suitcase in the trunk and held the passenger door for her.

"With so many children in your family, I guess I'm not surprised you are always punctual," he said as she settled in.

"My folks made a rule. If you weren't in the bathroom at your assigned time, it became open for whoever wanted it. My sisters loved to primp, so we learned early on not to be late."

"Uncle Hal used to say it was rude to keep people waiting," Cal said as he pulled back into traffic.

"It is. How are you coping with his being gone?" she asked gently.

"It's not as hard here. There's lots going on so I'm not thinking about it all the time. When in his home in Richmond, I expected him to appear every moment. It'll get easier. At least that's what people say."

"Easier, but the longing to see him, the wish for one afternoon again never quite fades," she said sadly.

"Speaking from experience?" he asked.

Zoe nodded.

"A dear friend died when we were in college. I still miss her."

Cal didn't speak again until Zoe gave directions for the steak house. Dinner didn't go as quickly as she had hoped since it was Friday night and the restaurant was crowded. By the time they finished their meal and were back on the road, it was after ten. They reached the cottage after eleven.

The wind blew from the ocean and the town of Seagrass Point was closed up. Few lights beyond streetlights illuminated the night. When they turned onto the road where the cottage sat, no lights showed at all.

"Not a lot of people live out here it seems," he said.

"Most of these places are summer homes. Which makes it ideal the rest of the year to get away. I love it when the beach is deserted and I can have it all to myself."

Once inside, Zoe hurried to turn on the heater.

"Fortunately my great-grandparents had hoped once to live year-round here so equipped the house for all weather. It'll warm up soon."

She stood in the living room and looked around, wondering what Cal saw. Could he imagine the years of loving visits from boisterous children and indulgent adults? Or did he see it as a casual home that showed its eclectic background and age?

"Shall I take the same bedroom as before?" he asked.

She nodded, breathing a soft sigh of relief. At least he wasn't going to pursue the matter he spoke of before. Maybe his idea of a honeymoon was different from hers.

"I left the water heater on when we left before, so if you want a shower, the water would be hot," she said, feeling a bit bewildered.

This wasn't quite turning out like she thought.

"I'd prefer to take one in the morning, after our run."

"Want hot chocolate or something before bed?" she asked.

"If you're making it, I'll have some. After I take our bags up to the rooms."

By the time the beverage was ready, the house had warmed enough Zoe could take off her jacket. Cal had returned after depositing the bags and lounged against the counter watching as she prepared the hot chocolate.

"I didn't see your laptop," she said, adding cocoa to the warming milk.

"Didn't bring it. But you reminded me," he said, taking his phone from his pocket.

He turned it off and laid it on the counter.

"No interruptions this time."

Zoe was startled. He was never incommunicado for work.

"What if someone needs you?"

"I'll be back in the office Monday morning. It can wait."

From the startled look on Zoe's face, Cal knew he'd surprised her. But he was serious about getting to know the woman he'd married.

He didn't see the need to tell her he'd reviewed her personnel file before coming this weekend. He figured he should know some of the basics, if only from the interview before he hired her. She was a graduate of Georgetown University. She'd worked as an analyst for two years for the Department of State and much preferred to work without close supervision. She'd received glowing reviews from her supervisor at State and had never given any trouble at Protection, Inc. Her insights were legendary. They worked well together, but this was different.

He didn't know what colors she liked, how she felt about discipline in children, or even names she'd want for their baby. Was she serious about staying home the first year, or would being with an infant all the time soon have her searching for adult companionship?

When Zoe handed him the mug of hot chocolate, he knew there were many more aspects he wondered about—how did she like to be kissed. How soft was her skin? Did she sleep snuggled up against a man or want her own space?

This weekend should answer a lot of questions.

Cal slept well and woke before dawn. He lay in bed a few moments considering all the things he would have done this weekend if he hadn't insisted on accompanying Zoe. Rising, he dressed in running clothes and went to see if she was awake.

Hearing movement in her room, he knocked. A moment later the door opened. She wore sweats and had her hair tied back into a ponytail.

"Ready?" he asked.

"I just need to put on my shoes. Aren't you going to be cold?"

He wore only shorts, shoes and a warm-up shirt. It would be cold starting out, but once he reached his stride, he'd be glad for fewer clothes.

"I'll be fine."

They did stretching exercises together. Cal was intrigued by the lithe body of his wife. He'd never noticed before. Or ever gone running with a woman. In the past, his social life was surface only. He was venturing into new territory.

The sun was just peeking above the horizon. The water was still more gray than blue. When they stepped outside, the breeze was cold. It wouldn't reach summer temperatures, but he hoped the sun would warm the day somewhat.

"Okay, I usually head north, where they're fewer houses," she said. "It doesn't really matter, the beach is deserted at this time of morning."

"And you like the loneliness of it," he guessed.

She shrugged. "I like to be by myself."

"Even now?"

"No, let's go."

They started out in tandem, he matching his pace to hers. Soon Zoe seemed to reach her stride. He could have pushed for more, but her pace was fast enough. They ran side by side, on the wet, packed sand. The ocean was on their right, sand dunes and houses on the left. Alone on the long expanse of seashore, they had the perfect place to run.

Cal relished the run. He'd been so caught up with work the last few days that he'd neglected his daily runs and missed them. A couple of days of this and he'd be back in top shape and raring to go back to work on Monday.

"This is two miles," Zoe said, slowing a bit and making a wide loop. "I usually run about four at a time."

"Works for me."

The time back seemed suspended. He noted the empty houses. The one house that had smoke coming from a chimney. Someone else up for the weekend. He wondered what Zoe would do in an emergency with so many empty places around.

He hadn't worried about anyone before. Now she was his wife. The only relative he had in the world. Would they really make a baby together, have a small son or daughter who would love the beach? To whom he could talk of his uncle Hal and growing up in Richmond?

The baby would have plenty of cousins on their mother's side. He'd encourage family ties even though he'd might never be included in many activities. Zoe would undoubtedly invite him, but everyone would know theirs wasn't a real marriage. Politeness wouldn't be the same as belonging.

Still, his child would be surrounded by love, both his and Zoe's.

He'd make sure of it.

Chapter Six

By the time they returned to the cottage, Zoe was getting winded and her hair was damp. Cal could have continued another mile, but stopped when she did. He liked running by the sea instead of in the park where he normally went. Maybe they could get away for more weekends and make this a part of their routine.

Wait a minute, he silently admonished himself. Don't get carried away with this. She was a wife only because he wasn't risking losing another child to a woman's whim. They had nothing in common except Protection, Inc. Getting married didn't mean *being* married in the traditional sense.

"Toss you for the shower first," she said, breathing hard.

"Does the water go cold after one shower?" he asked.

"Are you kidding? With all the people in my family, no one would ever get to bathe if one shower used up all the hot. Granddad put in a huge heater. It's enough for several showers in a row before the water even starts to cool down."

Too bad, Cal thought. He could have suggested they bathed together to save water.

"You go first. I'll do some more exercises out here and come in when you're finished," he said.

"Okay. I'll yell out the window when I'm done."

He watched her head into the house and shook his head. He was married to a woman so far from the pampered society darlings he'd dated that it was mind-boggling. He tried to picture any of the women he used to date yelling out a window.

An image of his uncle rose. Cal knew with certainty Hal would have liked Zoe.

Turning to face the sea, he dropped to do a series of pushups and then sit-ups. Might as well take the time to catch up on his physical exercises. It kept his mind off the tantalizing image of sharing a shower with Zoe.

When Cal came downstairs after his own shower, Zoe was curled up on the sofa leafing through a magazine. She looked up at him.

"Want to go out for breakfast? Or shall I make some pancakes?"

"I thought the idea was to remain hidden."

"Not hidden, just not out there, you know?"

He shook his head.

"We'll go to the pancake house in Waterford. It's not a far drive and I hardly ever go there so the chances of my mother's best friend spotting us are hugely remote."

"Where does your mother's best friend hang out?" Cal asked.

How far would Zoe go to keep their relationship quiet?

"Not anywhere near here, but you know what I mean. Anyone who knows her could ask who is the man her daughter is seeing. That would start speculation I don't need. Do you like pancakes?"

"Sure, who doesn't? We can stop at a grocery store later and get food for the rest of the weekend."

"You can make breakfast tomorrow and I'll do dinner tonight," she said, not looking at him.

Zoe wasn't sure how he'd take being treated like her brothers. She decided that was the best way to act. It was share and share alike in her family. She'd decided on the strategy to keep her sanity. If they could continue their relationship as they had done at work, she'd be able to handle things. If not, she was worried she'd make a blithering idiot of herself before the weekend was over.

"As long as you like omelets," he said.

"Who doesn't?" she parroted.

After breakfast, they walked around Waterford. It was a typical seaside resort—catering to tourists in the summer months, quiet and half empty in October.

The sun had warmed the day and being sheltered from the sea breeze by the buildings on Main Street kept the temperatures mild. They walked along gazing into shop windows, stopping inside a place or two. Zoe loved browsing driftwood sculptures. As far as she could tell, Cal had no special interests. But the way he kept watch, his eyes constantly assessing each place, she knew he was too busy figuring out ways he'd protect someone in this environment than in enjoying the sightseeing.

Crossing the empty street to the next block, Zoe saw a small boy standing by the shop door, looking scared.

"Think he's lost?" she asked Cal.

"Maybe." He stooped down to be on level with the little boy. "Where's your mom?" he asked gently.

The child gave a kind of hiccup and looked about to cry. "She's lost."

"Oh, dear," Zoe said.

Cal was hard-pressed to keep from smiling. It was this little tyke who was lost.

"Maybe we can find your mother. Where did you see her last?"

"I dunno," he said.

He stepped closer to Cal, looking at him trustingly.

"What's her name?" he asked, reaching out to place a reassuring hand on the child's shoulder.

"Mommy."

"I should have guessed. Shall we try this store first?" he asked.

The little boy looked at the door and wrinkled his nose.

"It smells in there."

"A clue," Cal said, straightening to his full height. "Maybe he was inside and didn't like the smell."

The store in question was a candle shop, with many different fragrances all competing on a whiff of air.

He felt a tug on his trouser pants. Looking down he smiled when he saw the earnest look on the boy's face.

"If you carried me, I could see better," he said.

Cal exchanged amused glances with Zoe, then hoisted the boy up. They entered the shop. It was much larger inside than it appeared from the sidewalk. There were many aisles, with shelves so tall people were concealed.

A woman near a register by the door glanced at them as they entered. Probably thought they were a family on an outing, Cal thought. If everything went well, in another year or two, that's exactly what they could be.

"We have a missing boy, here," Cal said to the clerk. "We are looking for his mother. Anyone report a missing child?"

"Oh, goodness, no. Where did you find him?"

"Right outside. He says this place smells, so we thought he might have come from here."

Just then a loud shriek sounded, followed by "Justin" being called very loudly.

The little boy broke into a smile.

"That's Mommy."

Two seconds later a frantic woman ran toward the front of the store, checking her speed when she saw her son.

"Oh, thank goodness," she said, rushing over. "You scared me to death."

"He was outside," Cal said, transferring the child to the frantic mother's arms. "Lucky he didn't wander farther away."

"I can't believe he left. I know he's tired of shopping. It's okay, honeybun. Mommy's finished for the day. Let's go get some ice cream."

She looked at Cal and Zoe relief clearly visible.

"Thank you for getting him. I don't want to even imagine if he had wandered down the street."

"Glad we were handy," Cal said.

Zoe smiled at the mother and at little Justin.

"You have a beautiful boy," she said.

The mother smiled proudly and nodded. "Thanks again."

Cal held the door for Zoe and they returned to the sidewalk.

"We can return to the cottage, if you like," she said when they stepped out.

"We haven't seen every place on the other side of the street," he said, glancing around.

"I knew it. You're bored."

The quiet lifestyle of this sleepy shore town wouldn't appeal to a man like Cal. He hobnobbed with business titans and heads of state.

He threw his arm around her shoulder and moved her closer to the wall to let another couple pass by.

"I'm not at all bored. I'm not interested in driftwood plant holders, or candles, but I am interested in the various ways people find to create products out of wax or what is essentially flotsam. This is a different kind of economy than I normally deal with, so it's fascinating people can actually make a living out of driftwood."

"Innovative, don't you think?"

Zoe hoped she didn't give herself away. She could scarcely think, only feel the warmth from his arm across her shoulder, and the blossom of hope in her heart for a baby. Cal would make such a great father.

He nodded, eyeing a particularly fanciful planter in the window.

"Where would someone put that?"

She tilted her head while looking at it, trying to breathe normally.

"I have no idea. On the porch of a beach cottage, I guess. I wouldn't take it home with me."

He took her hand, lacing his fingers with hers.

"You relieve my mind. Come on and let's find a sidewalk café by the water where we can get some coffee."

"We had coffee less than an hour ago."

She turned and fell into step with him. It felt special to be holding hands.

"I drink coffee all morning long, don't you?"

"Only days when I'm stressed."

"So today isn't one of them. Good. I still want coffee," he said.

They wandered down to the water's edge. The breeze was stronger near the sea. Anyone looking at them would believe they were lovers, out to explore a new place. She could almost believe it herself.

There were several docks with various types of boats bobbing against their ropes. More than one café dotted the block, but none had sidewalk seating this time of year.

"It's too cold to sit outside," Zoe said as they entered one establishment. "But come back in summer, every single place along this stretch of road has outside seating and we'd likely not find a spot."

"We could be awaiting the arrival of our child next summer."

Zoe swallowed and nodded, wishing there was some guarantee.

By the time they headed back to the cottage, clouds had moved in and the wind had changed directions, now blowing from the north. A storm looked inevitable.

"So much for a walk along the beach," Zoe said gazing at the gray sky. "It's going to pour."

"It'll keep most folks home tonight, So maybe we'll try a restaurant that's closer," Cal said.

Zoe looked at him. She had been doing him a disservice. She didn't want to explain Cal to her family, but she was entitled to see whomever she wished wherever she wished. Having dinner with someone didn't necessarily mean more than having dinner together. So what if someone saw them?

Cal had been very accommodating. She owed him better.

"We can try the seafood place on Main Street," she said. "And who cares what gossip makes it to my folks."

"Maybe none will."

Zoe was more concerned about the afternoon. Dinner wasn't for hours. What would they do in the meantime? Her imagination spiked.

As soon as they reached the cottage, Cal stood on the porch, watching the waves. "Find a couple of blankets and let's sit outside and watch the storm build."

Zoe liked the idea. She relished the power of Mother Nature and often sat on the covered porch during summer thunderstorms. No one else in the family cared to brave the elements at this time of year. Had she found a kindred spirit with Cal?

She ran upstairs and brought down two old quilts. They pulled the rattan love seat closer to the screen where they had an unimpeded view of the breakers. Sitting side by side, Zoe felt a spark of surprise when Cal tucked the quilt in around her and sat close, his thigh pressing against hers as he tucked the second quilt around his legs, his arms free.

"You'll get cold," she warned, feeling anything but cold herself.

"If I do I'll bundle up more. Or you can keep me warm," he said, reaching an arm around her shoulders and pulling her even closer. "Now, tell me all about Zoe Blackstone and her very large family."

They spent the afternoon talking about childhood memories and family vacations. Her stories were vastly different being one of several children. Sometimes Cal commented on how fortunate she was to have a large family.

She knew he missed his uncle. How odd to be the last of a family. She couldn't imagine it.

Time seemed to fly by. The rain came as expected, blowing enough to force them back from the screen. But not enough to drive them inside.

Zoe grew aware she spoke more than he did as the afternoon passed, but did glean facts she'd never known before. His experiences as an only child fascinated her. She loved hearing him talk about the quiet vacations he and his uncle had taken, how they celebrated holidays and birthdays.

She wished she'd met Hal. He must have been a special kind of man to raise his sister's child and give Cal such a good basis for growing into adulthood.

Dinner was pleasant, without anyone she recognized in the restaurant. She worried too much about rumors flying. She wasn't doing anything wrong, yet keeping secrets was making her paranoid. Once assured there was no one to relay details to her parents about the man she brought to the cottage, she relaxed and enjoyed the meal.

As they drew closer to finishing, Zoe grew more and more nervous. Cal said they should get the first time over with. She knew he was right—the longer they delayed, the harder it would be.

Not that making love with Cal would be difficult, but she'd never been one to indulge in casual sex, and didn't feel she knew him as well as she hoped she would before they slept together. She liked him, more and more as they got better acquainted. If she let herself, she'd fantasize about this very sexy boss. But she was trying to keep an even keel—made more difficult by the impending night.

Thinking about sleeping together had Zoe put down her fork. She couldn't eat another morsel the anticipation was so strong. She wanted to delay the return to the cottage. She wanted to go right now. She couldn't make up her mind.

"Had enough?" Cal asked.

"Yes," she said.

She should have stuck to her original plan to find a man to fall in love with, get married and have a baby. Only it wasn't always possible to find a husband on demand.

When they reached the cottage, Zoe could hardly think straight. She wasn't in this alone, Was Cal equally nervous? Glancing at him convinced her otherwise. She doubted anything bothered him. He was cool in crisis situations. And this hardly qualified as a crisis.

"Relax," he said, closing the cottage door behind him. "We're not going to do anything you don't want."

She jumped and turned to face him. He could read minds. Slipping out of her jacket, she let it fall onto a nearby chair, her gaze locked with his.

"I do want."

"I want more than just compliance for the bargain's sake," he said, stepping closer.

Gently he ran a finger along her cheek, tracing the jawline. She looked into his eyes, reassured by the desire she saw. He wanted her as much as she wanted him.

He leaned over and brushed his lips against hers. Pulling back he met her gaze again.

"Tell me when to stop," he said softly, brushing his lips along her jaw, giving short, sweet kisses along her throat, pausing at the pulse point at its base.

Never was about right, she thought as she closed her eyes to better savor Cal's lips against her skin. He put his hands on either side of her head, tilting it up slightly for his kiss—like a man kisses a woman he wanted. She was being seduced and it was heady stuff.

She felt a thrill of excitement and reached out to draw him

closer. Her heart pounded and blood rushed through her veins. It might be a bargain made, but she was not thinking of that now, but of the way Cal made her feel—special, cherished, sexy.

Slowly Cal began moving her toward the stairs. When they reached the bottom step, he lifted her into his arms and began to climb.

"I'm too heavy," she protested, secretly thrilled.

What woman didn't wish for some dashing man to sweep her off her feet and carry her away? When he didn't reply, she trailed light kisses along his jaw. The scratchy beard tantalized. She drew in a deep breath, savoring his scent. Her heart pounded so fast she knew he had to feel it.

When they reached the top, he was not even breathing hard. He looked at her.

"Are you sure?"

"Oh, yes," she said, gazing into his dark eyes.

She'd never felt so right about anything.

He nudged the door to her bedroom and stepped inside, slowly letting her slide from his arms until she stood pressed against him.

She liked the cocooning feeling. Just the two of them, together in the night.

"Come, share my bed," she whispered, leading him to the edge.

There was no going back.

Sunday morning the sound of rain on the roof woke Zoe. She rolled over and bumped into Cal. Opening her eyes, she looked at him in surprise, the memory of last night flashing into mind. He was still asleep.

For a moment she panicked. Then reason returned.

Taking advantage of the situation, she studied Cal as he slept, memorizing the way his eyebrows arched over his eyes, his lean cheeks, not softened by sleep. He could waken and be ready to go in an instant, she thought.

Slowly she eased from bed and snatched up a robe from a nearby chair. She gathered fresh clothes and headed for the bathroom to shower and dress.

What was the morning-after protocol? She should wait for him to waken. But that would prove too awkward. She'd feel more in control if she was dressed. And maybe had a couple of cups of coffee to bolster her confidence. She could have breakfast ready when he came down. That would be a wifely kind of thing to do.

The bathroom was cool. The outside temperature obviously dropped significantly last night. She'd have to turn up the furnace. As she stood beneath the hot water, she mentally ran through a checklist of all she wanted to do today, which helped her to keep from dwelling on last night. On every glorious touch, caress, kiss. It was amazing how much she craved his touch again. She tilted her face to the cascading water and tried to think of something else.

In a short time she was downstairs, dressed, and warm, the memories of their night accompanied her.

Preparing coffee, she heard the shower running and began to gather ingredients for an omelet. What time would Cal wish to return to Washington? She had things she could do to fill the hours if he wanted to leave after lunch. Glancing out the window, she wished it wasn't raining. A run on the beach would do wonders.

"Good morning," he said before she had gathered her thoughts.

"Hi. Coffee's ready."

Great opening, she thought. Should she kiss him? They'd made love far into the night and all she could think of was she hoped no one at work would find out. How did coworkers manage affairs?

"Up to a run this morning?" he asked, casually crossing the large kitchen and helping himself to a cup.

"It's pouring."

"You don't run in the rain?" he asked.

"Not when it's forty degrees. Summer rain, maybe."

"Then we'll have to find something else to do today."

The thought of going back to bed flashed into her mind. She turned away, testing the heat of the pan.

"I thought we'd return to Washington," Zoe said.

"Time enough tomorrow morning. If we leave early, we can arrive at the office before nine."

He crossed to her and put a finger beneath her chin, raising her face. Kissing her briefly, he looked deep into her eyes.

"I say we take today for ourselves and face the world again tomorrow."

"And do what all day? We have some books—"

He put his finger across her mouth.

"We start with breakfast and see where the day takes us."

Not a very good plan, Zoe thought as she began cooking, but she couldn't think very well when he was touching her.

Early Monday morning Cal drove them back to Washington. He'd originally planned to return on Sunday, but after Saturday night would not deny himself more time with Zoe. Saturday night she'd been responsive and passionate, which had surprised him. She was an outstanding analyst—

detailed, questioning, dissecting facts. He had superimposed that trait on all aspects of her life, but she'd proved him wrong in that regard.

She didn't analyze everything. She gave her entire being into the moment, making love with enthusiasm, holding nothing back.

He'd turned his phone on before they left the cottage and it had already rung twice. It rang again and he glanced at the caller ID. Emily. He'd better take this one.

"Yes?" he answered.

In no time his secretary began bringing him up to speed on various situations. He would have wished for more time to transition from the weekend at the cottage.

It had been relaxing and informative. He wanted to process what he learned about Zoe and figure out the best way to deal with each other over the years to come.

Refusing to admit he had enjoyed himself more than he'd hoped, he tried to catalog every aspect from running along the beach Saturday morning, to sitting on the porch while the rain isolated them, to strolling along the sidewalk in Waterford. He wouldn't forget the rather quiet weekend in a long time. There were too few respites like that in his life.

When Emily finally ran down, he assured her he was on his way in and would arrive at the office soon.

"We can go directly there if you like," Zoe said.

She'd been quiet during the drive and Cal had given up trying to gauge her mood.

"I can take time enough to drop you at your place," he offered.

There had been a slight awkwardness Sunday morning, but that had passed, only to appear again this morning. Was that going to be the pattern after every night together? He gave some thought to their moving in with each other. It would resolve the awkwardness and give them a chance to learn more about each other faster.

Would she be amenable to his suggestion?

What would it be like to make love to her each night? Wake up with her each morning? Share a home?

He'd always thought in the back of his mind he'd have children. But he'd never really envisioned being married or pictured the day-to-day details like eating breakfast together, sharing a bathroom, a bed.

He admitted a marriage like he envisioned would never have worked with Suzanne. Or any of the other women he'd dated over the years. He'd been on a fast track to get Protection, Inc. off the ground and build it up to the level it had attained. He liked taking beautiful women to places to show off, but in retrospect, they had all been too self-absorbed to be marriage material. But Zoe was different. He was learning they shared similar values. He liked being around her.

"I'm going to be pretty busy this week," Zoe said.

"At work?"

"And afterward. I have plans," she said, not looking at him.

So much for the idea they'd gone past the awkwardness or that she'd even consider moving in with him.

"Next weekend I'll be busy," Cal said. "I'm driving down to Richmond to start the sorting process. I don't want the house to sit empty for long. Want to go with me?"

"Um," she said.

"Is that a yes or no?"

"It's a I'm-trying-to-visualize-you-sorting-through-your-uncle's-things um."

"Why is that hard to do?"

"I'd think you'd hire someone to do it."

"No one can sort through family stuff except family."

Did she see him that detached, that he wouldn't care about his past?

"I agree, but I can't visualize you in a family situation, I guess. You are always so larger than life at work," Zoe said.

Cal glanced at her.

"I run a successful business, but that's not all I do or am."

"What else? You haven't mentioned any other current interests in our conversations. Getting you to talk about yourself is like pulling teeth. My brothers have no trouble monopolizing the conversation."

"I've learned to give little away. It makes it easer to keep safe."

"I'm hardly some terrorist or kidnapper."

She had a point.

"You know I ski in winter, sail in summer and guest speak at the local colleges and universities in law enforcement classes," he said.

"College classes?"

He nodded.

"There are electives in criminology for the latest techniques for keeping people safe in today's world. Guest-speaker status only. I have no intentions of becoming a professor."

"Wow, I'm impressed."

"I'm not out to impress you, merely letting you know more about me."

He rarely told people about his activities.

"We talked all weekend and you never once mentioned any of that, why not? You're too secretive, that's your problem."

"I didn't realize it was a problem keeping my life private," Cal said, his concentration split between Zoe and the heavy morning traffic.

"Not at work, maybe, but shouldn't I know more about my baby's father than what every other employee at work knows?"

"Your husband, you mean?"

"Um, that, too."

"You drive me crazy with your ums. Do I need an interpretive guide?"

She laughed and Cal felt pleasure at amusing her.

He'd spent more of the weekend finding out about Zoe and her family than talking much about his. He'd spoken of the past, the vacations with his uncle, but not much about his life since he'd become an adult. He was a private person. No one could find a chink in his armor if they didn't know much about him.

He pulled into the parking garage of the high-rise building where the offices were located.

"I'll get a cab home, if you'll drop off my bag next time you pass my apartment," Zoe said, getting out of the car. "Saves dealing with them now."

"I'll drive you home tonight," he said, looking at her across the roof of the car.

"I told you, I have plans."

She turned and began walking toward the elevator at a brisk pace. Cal said a brief expletive and locked the car, lengthening his stride until he caught up with her. Taking her arm, he stopped her.

Zoe looked at his hand and then up to his face.

"What?"

"You can't walk off like that. I'll take you home so you'll have your car for your secretive plans."

"They aren't secretive, they just don't include you."

Cal suddenly wanted to know what she was doing. Was that a prick of jealousy? He didn't like the idea. She was free to do what she wanted. As was he.

Only he had no plans for the evening. What was she going to do?

"You might need some of the things in your suitcase this evening," he said.

What was he doing? Trying to find out what she was up to? If he wanted that intel there were ways to find out.

"I don't."

She pulled her arm away and glanced to her left. One of the women from the secretary pool was walking rapidly toward them.

She eyed them warily and continued to the elevator. Turning, she watched as both he and Zoe looked at her. No one said a word. When the doors opened, Zoe stepped forward. He reached out again.

"Wait," he said.

The elevator doors closed behind the secretary.

"I have work to do," she said, still staring at the closed elevator.

"I do, as well. But we haven't settled this."

She swung around and faced him.

"Settled what?"

"Us."

She frowned. "What do you mean?"

"I think we should move in together."

"What? Whatever for?"

"It's not always going to be convenient to run out to the sea cottage every time we want to sleep together."

"Shhh."

She glanced quickly around the garage, then stepped closer. "Keep your voice down. Do you want the entire world to know what we're doing?"

For a moment Cal almost said yes.

"I'm trying to look at this from a practical point of view," he said evenly.

"Living together wasn't part of the bargain. I went along with your condition of marriage, but living together isn't in the cards. Now I do have to get to work before we cause any more gossip than what Sally Ann is probably spreading at this very moment."

"Sally Ann?"

"The secretary who just passed. Who knows what she heard?"

"Nothing the entire world couldn't hear."

Cal turned and walked beside her to the elevator.

The weekend wasn't ending as he thought it would. He couldn't force her to move in with him. And he couldn't go to her place unless she invited him. What a mess.

He needed time to think of a new strategy.

Zoe closed the door to her office with relief. She couldn't do this. She had given it her best shot this weekend, but sleeping with the boss was more than she could deal with. Especially when they weren't even having an affair but were solely bent on having a baby. Too totally weird.

How could he have suggested they move in together? She'd barely made it through the weekend. She could never live day after day with Cal. She'd do something totally foolish like fall for him and come to expect more than he could deliver.

She had to keep the relationship focused on the end goal. Nothing more.

She went to her desk and opened her calendar. It wasn't her most fertile time. She was due to start her period in a few days. So most likely, no baby this month.

The thought of making love with Cal again and again until she did conceive had her giddy. She thought she could be sophisticated about it, but she couldn't. Picking up the phone, she quickly dialed her twin's number.

"Chloe here."

"Hey, are we still on tonight?" Zoe asked.

"Sure. I tried calling you this weekend. Where were you? Even your cell was off."

"I went to the beach," she said.

"With Cal?"

"Yes."

"And?"

She couldn't tell her sister everything. Chloe would never have gone for a bargain like theirs. But it felt odd holding anything back from her twin.

"And it was wonderful," she said truthfully. "Rain and all."

"Especially the rain, I bet. Nothing like forced confinement to find some other way to spend the day," Chloe teased. "I expect a full report at dinner. Let's meet at the rib place."

"Sounds good. Can you give me a lift home? I don't have my car. We came straight in to the office from the cottage."

"Better and better. I bet you didn't want to leave. Sure. Gabe's out of town again, so I'm footloose and fancy free. See you at six."

So which was worse, Zoe wondered, the inquisition by her sister or seeing Cal again? She hoped work could keep her mind from dwelling on either.

Zoe made it through the week without a confrontation with either her sister or husband-in-name-only. Cal had dropped off her small suitcase at her apartment on Monday while she'd been at dinner with Chloe.

By carefully arriving at work each morning after she knew Cal was there, Zoe avoided seeing him unless he called a meeting. She always left promptly at five to head off any chance of an after-work encounter.

Friday morning she wasn't feeling well. She knew her period was about to start and knowing what to expect, took a handful of pills. Sometimes she could head off the pain if she acted early enough. There was too much to do to take another day off. If this could only have waited another twenty-four hours, she could stay in bed all day Saturday.

By midafternoon, Zoe had to leave for home. She could barely stand upright the pain was so intense. Driving wasn't easy, but knowing the sooner she got home, the sooner she could get some relief made it possible. Almost doubled up by the time she reached her apartment, she headed right for the bathroom and more of the pills she'd taken that morning.

Changing into an old flannel nightie that was loose and soft, she crawled into bed and curled into a ball. No baby on the way. For a moment tears threatened. She fought against them. She knew it would be a long shot to get pregnant at all, much less the first time. Still, she had hoped.

Once the analgesic took effect, she dozed off.

The phone woke her.

"Hello?"

If it were Chloe, she'd ask her to come over. She would like something to eat but couldn't face making anything herself.

"Are you coming with me to Richmond?" Cal asked.

She'd forgotten he'd asked her last Monday and she'd never answered. They'd gotten sidetracked.

At least she hadn't heard any gossip this week. Maybe Sally Ann had more discretion that Zoe thought.

"Not this weekend," she said, barely suppressing a moan.

"What are you doing?"

"Right now I'm curled up in a ball trying to fight the pain," she said.

"Cramps?"

"That's an understatement. I can hardly stand, much less take some car trip to Richmond. You don't need me. It's your family estate."

"I'll be right over."

"No, I—"

She was speaking to an empty line. He had hung up.

Great,exactly what she didn't need. If she ignored the door when he rang the bell, maybe he'd go away.

Not if she knew Cal. He was more likely to get the landlord and have him open the door, claiming she was too ill to reach the door. Cal never made things easy.

Yet she was touched he was coming to see her. Once he'd seen there was nothing he could do, he'd be off to Richmond.

For a few precious moments, she felt cherished. Odd from such a solitary, independent man.

She got up and splashed water on her face. Donning a robe, she went into the living room and curled up on the sofa to await Cal. In less than ten minutes he knocked on the door.

Opening it she leaned against it and looked at him.

"I can manage," she said.

"I'm sure you can," he said, walking past her and reaching back to shut the door. "But you don't have to manage alone. What do you need?"

"Relief," she said, holding her abdomen.

It felt as if a dozen knives were cutting into her.

"You're as pale as snow," he said, studying her for a moment.

"I have some pain medication. Which doesn't completely block it."

Zoe walked to the sofa and sank down on it, bringing her knees up and encircling her legs with her arms. This was the best position for the maximum relief. The only thing to do was ride it out.

He looked momentarily helpless. It was odd seeing Cal with that expression. She always thought he could handle anything from terrorists, to members of Congress, even foreign dignitaries who demanded so much attention.

But here was something no one could do anything about until she saw the surgeon.

"Thanks for stopping by, but there's nothing you can do. I'll be back to work on Monday, most likely. You go on to Richmond."

Cal shook his head.

"I'm staying. Have you eaten?"

When she shook her head, he glanced toward her kitchen. "Want an omelet?"

"That sounds nice," she said.

It'd give him something to do and she was hungry. It'd be nice to have something more substantial than a cup of soup, which was all she felt like preparing.

She leaned back and closed her eyes as she listened to him work in her kitchen. She didn't have any pets due to her erratic work hours. She'd moved out on her own once she could afford it with the then new position at Protection, Inc. She was used to being alone so it felt strange to hear him in the other room.

She wondered how she'd adjust to being married—if it had been a real marriage. The give and take of sharing a space with someone. Learning his habits as he learned hers. Growing together until the sounds the other made would be normal, and being alone wouldn't be.

Cal had suggested they move in together. She'd have to explain to everyone in her family about the wedding if not the reason for it. Too much trouble to change things back if she couldn't have a baby. Better to leave things as they were. But she did appreciate the help, much as she valued her independence.

He wasn't going to use this as more leverage to try to get her to agree to moving in together, was he?

Chapter Seven

Cal took off his suit coat and laid it across one of the stools in the kitchen. Hunting through the cupboards and refrigerator, he found the ingredients and pan he needed. How unobservant had he been not to notice a pattern of her missing work on a monthly basis? Did she normally suffer through the pain to remain sharp, or had most instances occurred on the weekend when she could take pain meds that made her groggy? If he hadn't wanted her to go to Richmond, would he even have known she left early and was in such discomfort? Probably not.

So much for being in tune with his employees.

When the meal was ready, he found a tray and carried the plates into the living room.

"Are you asleep?" he asked.

She shook her head and opened her eyes.

"I wish I could. Sooner or later I'll be too tired to stay awake. This looks good. Thank you."

He sat opposite her in one of the surprisingly comfortable chairs. Glancing around the room, he noted the way she decorated. The warmth was not unexpected coming from Zoe. Quite a change from Suzanne's black and white sleek ultramodern apartment.

He frowned. He didn't want to be reminded of that woman.

"Mine is good, isn't yours?" Zoe asked.

He looked at her. "What?"

"You made a face. Isn't your omelet good?"

"It's fine."

He hadn't even noticed the taste as he ate—too preoccupied with the past. There was nothing he could do now except hope for a better future. One that included a child or children.

"Would your getting pregnant change things for you, so you could get pregnant again?" he asked.

She shook her head.

"Probably not as I understand things. I never really thought about it, but in the back of my mind, I guess I always expected to have a bunch of kids. Maybe not as many as Mom and Dad did, but more than one. Now I'd be very grateful for one."

They ate in silence. When finished, Cal quickly cleaned up over Zoe's protests. Rejoining her in the living room a short time later, he sat beside her on the sofa.

"You don't have to stay," she said.

"I think you need to give more thought to my idea of moving in together. If you don't get pregnant in the next few weeks, you'll need help the next time this happens."

She knew it.

"Cal, I've managed for years with this. I can handle it."

"Except you don't need to handle it alone anymore. You have a husband now."

She smiled.

"You take your husbandly duties very seriously. We're not

really married."

"Yes, we are."

"Not in the traditional sense, I mean. You're not responsible for me."

"I want to take care of my baby's mother."

She studied him a moment.

"Would you have married Suzanne if she hadn't aborted the baby? Did she need taking care of?"

"She wanted marriage without any babies. I wasn't ready to commit to her. Perhaps subconsciously I knew what kind of woman she is. But, yes, if she'd continued the pregnancy, I probably would have married her."

He didn't want to think of what kind of marriage they would have had. Parties every weekend, shopping expenditures spending thousands of dollars, vacations in exotic locales. There'd have been no longtime family sea cottage.

And he suspected Suzanne didn't deal with family problems well. She'd been convenient for the social scene. But he'd never thought about marriage around her.

He looked at Zoe. He'd never thought about marriage with her, either. But now he admitted to being oddly content. Logically it made sense to move in together. Why didn't she see that?

"If you'd leave, I could go to bed," she said.

"Go to bed if you like. I hardly need entertainment."

She eyed him.

"You brought your laptop?"

"It's in the car."

He could see her debating the merits of leaving him and going back to bed.

"Go on, Zoe. I'll stay for a little while in case you need anything."

She nodded and rose, heading for the back of the apartment, bent over and walking slow. He hadn't seen her bedroom and wondered if it was frilly and feminine or more tailored. Should he have carried her back to bed?

He didn't like not being able to fix things.

He went to his car and got his laptop, letting himself back in the door he'd left unlocked. The apartment was silent. He walked down the hall and peeped in the room. She was sleeping. With a glance around to satisfy himself on her room, he returned to the kitchen to make some coffee. Opening his laptop a few moments later, he began searching the Internet for information on Zoe's condition.

The next morning Cal woke at first light. He'd bunked down on the sofa again. He walked down the short hall and peeked into the bedroom. Last night he'd checked on Zoe a second time before going to sleep. She'd been sound asleep and he hoped she'd been able to sleep through the night undisturbed. She was still curled up under the covers, only the top of her head visible. That was a good sign, wasn't it?

Taking a quick shower, he wished he'd thrown a change of clothes in the car. He could go a day without shaving, but he hated putting on the same shirt he'd worn the day before.

He was leaving the bathroom when he heard the front door open. Stepping into the living room almost at the same time as Zoe's twin did, Cal knew Chloe hadn't suspected he was in residence.

"Oh, you startled me," Chloe said when she spied him. "What are you doing here?"

"Zoe's not feeling well," he said easily.

"I know. She called me yesterday and left a message on my machine. I didn't get it until late. I thought I'd come by to fix her breakfast."

Start as you mean to go on had been the adage his uncle Hal had been fond of. Good advice.

"We can make it together. I was just heading to the kitchen," he said.

Cal saw no reason to leave just because Chloe had arrived.

"How's Zoe?" she asked.

"Slept through the night, I think."

Chloe looked so much like Zoe Cal was continually fascinated. They even wore their hair in the same style. Didn't most twins try to look different from each other? Or were they so used to the similarity they didn't notice it?

"Sleep's the best thing. I'll help with breakfast and you and I can get to know each other better," she said, taking off her jacket.

Cal felt a spark of amusement at her challenge. He had no siblings but recognized the loyalty of a family bond when he saw it.

"Sounds like a plan."

By the time pancakes and sausages had been prepared, Cal knew Chloe a bit better. She seemed easier to get along with than Zoe, but maybe she was on her best behavior. Also, he wasn't married to her and trying to get her to give in to his idea of sharing an apartment.

When the food was ready, Chloe went to check on her sister. She returned a moment later.

"She's awake and hungry, which is good. Sometimes she doesn't eat for two or three days."

He took a plate and piled pancakes and sausage on it.

"She's hungry, but not that much," Chloe said with a smile, taking off a couple of pancakes and one link of sausage.

"You look like Zoe when you do that," he commented.

"I prefer to think she looks like me," she replied, lifting the tray and heading for her sister's room.

When she returned a short time later, Cal had finished his coffee.

"I'm heading home to change and get a few things. Will you stay with her until I get back?"

"You don't need to come back, I'll stay the weekend. Gabe is away."

"I'll be back as soon as I pick up a few things," he said, deliberately leaving his laptop on the table and heading out a few moments later.

Chloe prepared a cup of coffee and wandered back to her sister's room. Zoe had eaten half the food and was curled up staring out the window.

"That man is determined to act the role of husband," Chloe said, sitting carefully on the foot of the bed.

"Cal? Is he still here?"

"No, he left. But he's coming back. And I'm not sure I'd try to keep him out when he does."

Zoe made a face.

"He gets this strong sense of responsibility. I told him I could manage on my own. I thought he was going to Richmond this weekend to start winding up his uncle's affairs."

Zoe told Chloe about Cal's uncle and a brief history of his childhood.

"Sounds like you're his family now," Chloe mused.

"Just until I have a baby. If I can't conceive, then he'll look elsewhere."

Chloe took a sip of her coffee.

"So conceive."

Zoe laughed softly.

"As if it were that easy."

Her expression changed.

"What if I can't?"

"Then you'll deal with it. Don't give up before trying. You've only been on this quest a few weeks.

"I'm in so much pain I don't know how many more months I can take before I have to give in for that operation," Zoe said. "That's depressing. Change the subject. Tell me about your latest listing. Give me something else to think about."

"It's a fabulous house, simply beautiful from the outside and fantastic on the inside," Chloe began. She talked about other homes she'd been showing to clients. When she saw Zoe had fallen back asleep, she slipped from the bedroom.

Cal packed a small bag with essentials and included a couple of pairs of casual pants, several shirts. He swung by a florist's and picked out a bouquet of mums in fall colors. They should brighten Zoe up a bit. He'd get her chocolate as well, but had a feeling she was too ill to enjoy them.

He shook his head with the thought. He acted like he was courting

One last stop when he swung by the office on the way back to Zoe's apartment. Picking up some files, he'd keep them in reserve in case he had time to work while she rested. He knew she didn't want him there, but something compelled him.

Chloe opened the door to his knock.

"Pretty flowers. I told her you'd be back. She's asleep. It's the best thing for her. I think there are vases beneath the sink. I'd stay, but you have things under control. I put my number by the phone in the kitchen in case you need to get in touch with me."

He nodded. He couldn't think of a reason he'd need her, but if it made her feel better, he'd go along with it.

It was quiet when she left. He found the vase and filled it with water. Taking off the wrapping paper, he stuck the flowers in. They were bunched together and looked bright and cheerful. He quietly walked to her room. She was sleeping, her face slightly flushed. Placing the vase on the nightstand, he left as quietly.

Cal made a space for himself at the dining table, powered up his laptop and went to work.

Zoe woke late afternoon feeling better. She breathed a sigh of relief. Most likely the worst was behind her for this month. Stretching, she noticed the flowers beside the bed. Mums were such a fall flower. She loved them. These were burnt-orange, bright yellow and a pale cream. Lovely. She was feeling pampered.

She rose and went to the bathroom, taking a leisurely shower. Dressing in loose-fitting pants and a warm sweatshirt with bunnies on the front, she wandered out to get something to eat. She stopped suddenly when she realized Cal sat at her dining table. She'd thought herself alone in the apartment.

"What are you doing here?" she asked.

He glanced at her.

"Feeling better?"

"Much. I thought you left hours ago."

"I did. I went home to get a few things. I came back before your sister left. Need anything?"

"The flowers are from you?"

He nodded, watching her closely.

She smiled, surprised.

"Thank you, they're lovely."

"Need anything else?"

"Nothing I can't get myself. Go on home, Cal."

"I'm staying," he said calmly. "Cute bunnies."

Zoe glared at him, but Cal merely returned her stare with an amused one of his own. She considered demanding he leave, but had a suspicion he'd ignore her.

Continuing to the kitchen, Zoe set about preparing tea and some muffins. She tried to appreciate his willingness to help, but she didn't need it or him. Even her sister knew better than to crowd her space. Yet the more she thought about it, the more she was touched he stuck around.

Once her light meal was ready, she carried it into the living area. She could demand he move and let her use the table, but she'd just as soon eat the snack on the sofa. Still, she wanted to do something to assert her rights in her own place.

He looked at her.

"Is that enough?"

"For now. I'll eat more for dinner if I still feel okay."

"I'm starting to realize how severe these attacks can be," he said, rising and coming to sit beside her on the sofa.

"Doctors don't recommend surgery lightly," she said, feeling as if he took up more than his share of space.

She couldn't move without being obvious, but he seemed too close. Glancing down she saw there was more than a foot of sofa between them.

"All the more reason to see if you can get pregnant as quickly as possible," he said.

She could feel herself grown warm with embarrassment. She wasn't comfortable discussing sex with Cal. It was one thing to relive every moment at night when she was alone in her bed, or during a break at work, but the thought of shedding her clothes and his and making love again was more than she could casually handle with him so close.

"Be easier if we lived together," he continued. "We wouldn't be limited by a trip to the cottage."

"Okay, you have made your point several times. I agree for when I'm fertile. But other than that, there's no reason to."

She'd make any concession to get him to stop pressing her on the matter. She needed to maintain her independence.

He studied her for a moment.

"When you're ready my place is bigger. I have two bedrooms. You'd have more privacy."

"Fine."

"So when do you think you'll move in?" he asked.

Was there a hint of self-satisfaction in his tone. Zoe frowned. She felt pressured.

"In a week or so."

Once there she imagined there'd be nightly bouts of sex. She almost caught her breath at the thought. She'd loved the two nights at the cottage. She just wished there was a bit more to their relationship. All intimacy required some time to develop. Physically they had been as intimate as two people could be, yet he held so much in reserve, she didn't feel close to him as she'd like. Did he feel that way about her?

"I hope you have a streaming service. I thought we could watch some movies this evening."

"You don't have to stay."

"And miss the movies?"

The rest of the weekend passed uneventfully. Cal left Sunday morning after she assured him she was past the worst. Still feeling shaky after her bout she didn't do much that day beyond reading and going for a short walk. But at least she got out of the apartment.

Always in the back of her mind was the thought of moving in, temporarily, with Cal in a few days. What would it be like to share a space with him?

Monday at work, Cal called to check on her. She was busy and quickly told him she was fine.

Tuesday he stopped by her office for a moment.

Wednesday he had Emily call in the afternoon.

Thursday he stopped by as Zoe was ready to leave.

"Going home?" he asked, leaning against the doorjamb.

"Yes. I'm fine, Cal, as I've told you every day this week."

"When are you coming to my place?"

She hesitated a moment, taking time to button her coat. It was cold outside.

"In a few days. Next weekend."

She dare not procrastinate beyond her optimum fertile time. Yet she felt as shy as a schoolgirl around him these days. She had to shake that feeling off and get on with the business of having a baby.

Looking at him, she made her decision.

"Saturday."

"Then let's go out to dinner tonight or tomorrow. Early Saturday, I'll help you move your things to my place," he suggested.

"I'm only bringing a few clothes, not moving," she protested.

"Want to go to the cottage afterward?" he said, ignoring her comment.

"Don't you have to go to Richmond to sort things?"

"It can wait a little longer. I've decided to rent the house for the time being. I can always sell it later if I want. I'll need to get it cleared before I list it with a rental agency. But there's no great rush."

"This way you keep it in the family longer," she said.

It showed a surprising sentimental streak in the man. She hadn't expected that.

"Who knows, our son or daughter may wish to live in Richmond when grown."

Her heart skipped a beat with his casual mention of their child.

"What are you worried about?" he asked.

She was surprised he'd picked up on how she felt.

"Nothing."

"Something."

He pushed away from the door and walked across the office to stand beside her. Leaning over, he brushed his lips against hers. She jumped back.

"That's it, isn't it. You don't like me touching you."

"I like it."

She could get to like it too much.

"It feels rushed. I know it is, because of time. I feel funny about it all."

"So spending time together will help you feel more at ease, right?"

"I guess."

"Then come to dinner with me tonight."

She debated. He had a point: if she felt more comfortable around him, things would be easier.

Only, she was afraid getting too comfortable would mean she might grow to care for him more than he wanted.

Still, this was only dinner.

"All right."

She nodded, watching him speak, wondering when he would kiss her again. Far from disliking his touch, she was really afraid she'd grow to like it too much.

Cal took her to a grill near the capitol on Thursday evening. The food was delicious and due to the dearth of customers, the service was excellent. Once they'd been served, Zoe glanced around.

"I haven't been here before. Is it a favorite of yours?"

"It's my second time. I came with a couple of men from work a few months back and we enjoyed it."

She cast around for another topic of conversation, smiling when she had the perfect question.

"Tell me about growing up in Richmond. We grew up in the District, so how did living in Virginia compare?"

"Probably similar. Played cowboys and Indians when young, sports as a teen."

"We all played sports in high school. Which ones, basketball or baseball?"

He looked at her in amusement.

"Is this an inquisition?"

She shrugged.

"Sort of. You know lots about me, but I still don't know a great deal about you. What was your favorite sport?"

"Baseball in spring, football in fall, pickup games of all

kinds in summer."

"Not basketball? You're tall enough," she asked.

"I played in school but didn't care about it one way or another."

"What did you do best in school?"

"Math."

She blinked.

"I'm surprised. Why aren't you an accountant?"

He laughed at that.

"Merely because I was good at it didn't mean I wanted to deal in numbers all day long. What were you best in?"

"History."

"So, why not be an historian or a teacher?"

"Good point. I love what I do, actually. I find it more fascinating than any other job I can think of."

"Me, too. The training I received in the Army enabled me to open Protection, Inc. There are new programs and training courses I take all the time to keep on top of the field. Trying to outwit others is intriguing enough for any man."

"Keeping people safe is important. It's a rough world these days. Did your uncle approve of your career?"

"He wanted me to do what made me happy."

"Is that how you feel about our child, he or she can do whatever as long as they're happy?"

"Within reason. No bank robbery no matter how happy that makes him."

Zoe was surprised at his teasing note. She associated Cal with being serious, focused, aware of everything going on around him.

It reiterated her point that she didn't know him all that well.

"So tell me about your best friend in school," she said.

"Jason is still probably my closest friend. He and I have gone through a lot together."

Cal began to tell her stories of two young boys growing up. Much of what he related sounded like her own brothers and their friends. She laughed from time to time. She suspected Cal was embellishing things.

This side of him intrigued her. Was he actually flirting with her? In a low-keyed, Cal sort of way?

The mealtime passed swiftly. She was sorry when it was time to leave.

"Come in for some coffee or hot chocolate," she invited when they reached the door to her apartment a short time later.

"I have to be in the office early tomorrow for a call from London, so I'll take a rain check," Cal said.

He cupped her face in his palms and kissed her.

Zoe returned the kiss, open to his gentle pressure. She knew he was trying to make things easier between them and she needed to get over being shy, but all rational thought fled with the touch of his lips to hers.

He moved his hands to pull her into a hug all the while kissing her. She wrapped her arms around his neck and returned his kiss with full measure.

A few moments later both were breathing hard and she forgot about coffee and wanted a bed where they could continue what they started. Forget about making a baby. She wanted Cal and she didn't much care if he knew that at the moment.

When he pulled back, she took a deep breath.

"Come in and stay the night," she said.

He considered for a moment.

"I have an early call from London."

"So leave early, really, really early."

She turned and fumbled for the door. He reached around her, took the keys and opened it.

Entering the dark apartment, he stopped her from turning on a light. Slipping her coat from her shoulders, he shut the door behind them and brought her back into his arms.

Cal kissed her again, enjoying her passionate response. He'd sensed the reserve in her before and had to find some way around it. Her response was all he could hope for.

Slowly he savored every taste, every move she made. He liked the small sounds she gave, almost like humming, or purring. She didn't pretend, but let him know exactly what she found delightful and what pleased her.

He hadn't planned for this, but since she seemed to be as involved as he was, he wasn't stopping. The apartment was faintly illuminated from the outside, buildings in Washington still lighted even though it was after ten. There was enough to enable him to move them toward the hallway without running into furniture.

Zoe kissed him back, running her hands over his shoulders, around his neck, her fingers combing through his hair. She was a bundle of soft curves, fitting into his embrace perfectly. Sweet and soft and feminine, not exhibiting any inhibitions.

Kisses were no longer enough. He wanted all of her.

When they reached the bedroom, he stopped for a moment, tilting up her face to see her in the dim light.

"Are you sure?" he said hoarsely.

He'd hate to stop, but the bigger picture was more important. If she wasn't ready, he would stop.

"Yes, are you?" she said, her voice breathless and sexy.

"Oh, yes," he said, kissing her again.

His hands tangled with hers as they removed clothing. Shirts dropped to the floor. The feel of her heated skin was heaven. He trailed kisses across her shoulders, along the tops of her breasts. She was warm and sweet and he wanted her more than he had ever wanted another woman. And for a moment, that scared the bejeesus out of him.

Slowly he lowered her on the bed and came down beside her. The timing was off for a baby, but not for a night of love.

Chapter Eight

Cal hated to leave before dawn. Zoe was asleep, curled next to him, one hand on his arm. He woke early, knowing he'd have to hustle to get home, shower and change and make it to work before the call came through. But he didn't want to move.

He took a breath, smelling the perfume she wore. Or was it her own special scent? He wished it were light enough to see her sleeping. He remembered how she'd looked at the cottage one morning. Her eyelashes were long and thick. Her cheeks had held faint color. Her hair had been tousled and spread across the pillow.

He sucked in another breath and slipped from the bed. Any further reminiscing and he'd never leave.

The streets were almost empty of traffic, it was too early for the morning commute to be in full swing. He made it to his flat in record time, trying to focus on the aspects of the important call, but his mind kept drifting back to Zoe.

Tomorrow she was moving into his flat. He wouldn't have to leave in the cold dark of predawn in the future. He could have those extra minutes he'd wanted. He knew he'd offered the second bedroom, but either she'd sleep in his, or he'd sleep in hers. A year ago having a baby was the farthest thing from his mind. Now his uncle was dead, Suzanne was no longer in the picture and the most important goal he could go for right now was having a baby with Zoe.

And then what?

Cal took a quick shower, shaved and dressed in under twenty minutes, focused on the call coming in, he deliberately turned his mind away from thinking about the future. Time enough to think about that after the baby was born.

When Zoe woke, she was alone. Lying in bed to claim a few more minutes before she had to get up, she began to think about what she'd agreed to. She wasn't at all sure she should have said she'd move into Cal's apartment. They were playing with fire, trying to build a relationship with the chance of having a child together not a sure thing.

What was he going to do if they tried for months and nothing happened? She couldn't go on forever dealing with the pain. Sooner or later she had to take her doctor's advice. It was early yet—she couldn't say she'd given getting pregnant much of a chance so far. But she was becoming more involved with Cal and if things didn't cool down a bit, she was afraid of what might happen.

Not that she thought Cal would give any complaints.

She worried about her own feelings—what if she fell in love with the man? It wasn't a bad thing to love a baby's father, but usually that came about before a baby was born—and the feeling was shared.

When she arrived at work, she put the matter from her mind. There were a flurry of notes on her normally cleared desk. The situation in the Balkans was heating up again and they had an operative there guarding from an assassination attempt. She scanned the messages and began calling up every scrap of recent information she had on the politician they were guarding, and the terrorist activities in the area.

Shortly after nine, Emily called her.

"Cal wants to see you."

"I'm busy right now," Zoe said, glancing between her computer screen and the notes she jotted down a couple of weeks ago.

"He's leaving soon. He says he needs to see you now," Emily said.

"Leaving? Okay, I need to talk to him anyway. I'll be right there."

She gathered some notes and a printout of the latest AP report of activity in the area and headed for Cal's office.

"Go on in," Emily said when Zoe arrived. "He doesn't have much time."

Zoe opened the door and stepped inside.

Cal was putting files into a briefcase. He glanced up when she entered.

"Close the door," he said, reaching for another stack of papers.

"What's up?" Zoe asked.

"That call from London changes a few things. I need to get to Europe."

"I brought intel on the situation in the Balkans. Is that why you're going?"

He looked up at that.

"No. What's going on there?"

She brought him up to speed and handed him the papers she'd brought. He glanced at them and stuffed them in his briefcase.

"Emily made reservations for an early afternoon flight to

London. I barely have time to get home to grab some clothes before I have to be at Dulles."

"How long will you be gone?" Zoe asked.

"I'm not sure."

She watched him. He seemed to have all he needed. He opened his drawer and pulled out his passport.

"That's everything," Cal said, putting it in his inside coat pocket.

He looked at her again.

"I'll do my best to be back in time."

"You could be gone for a week or longer?"

They hadn't considered him being gone during her fertile time.

"I have no idea," he said.

"What is going on?"

"Some things I can't discuss right now. I'll let you know when I can."

He came around the desk stopping beside her.

Zoe knew it was selfish to think of herself at a critical time like this. Cal didn't up and jaunt off to Europe without a moment's notice unless it was extremely important. But he couldn't even tell her if he'd be back when she'd need him.

She shook her head impatiently. She sounded like some farmer trying to breed a cow or something. He hadn't built a stellar company by neglecting client needs.

"Go. If you don't make it back in time, there's always next month," she said.

"And the one after, if we don't succeed next time. Take care of yourself," he said.

She nodded, holding her breath. Was he going to kiss her?

Emily tapped on the door and opened it without waiting.

"Here's the info on your flight. Let me know when to reserve a return."

She handed him a folder with the itinerary on top.

"This has all you requested. When you get there, call if you need anything else. I'll hang around tonight until I hear from you."

"I'll call you at home if I need anything," Cal said.

He glanced at Zoe, said goodbye and then left.

"Whew, we haven't had that tight a schedule in a while," Emily said. "I was afraid I wouldn't find available space today. It's surprising how full the flights are this time of year. Who wants to go to Europe in October?"

"Let me know if I can help in any way," Zoe said.

She returned to her office, curious as to the emergency, yet more concerned about Cal. He wasn't going into danger, was he?

The following days seemed to fly by. The situation in the Balkans was worsening. Several of the analysts conferred and finally made the recommendation to get the client to a safer country. It was a wise move. Their field operative and the client were no sooner in Brussels than the airport closed in the troubled city. If they'd waited, it might have been too late.

But that wasn't the situation Cal was dealing with, Zoe realized. What else was going on in Europe that required his presence?

Each day she crossed off the date on her calendar. She hadn't spoken to Cal since he'd been gone. There was enough to do with all the other situations, but she wished she could have talked to him at least once when he checked in with Emily.

By Friday evening, Zoe still didn't know when Cal might

return. She stopped by Emily's desk on her way out, but his secretary had left early to make up for long hours earlier in the week.

Shortly after arriving home, and changing, she called Chloe.

"Hi. What's up?"

"I was wondering what you are doing tonight," Zoe said.

She wanted to talk to someone. Who better than her twin?

"Gabe and I are cooking on the grill. Come on over, I'll add another steak. We plan a lazy evening doing nothing."

"Would I be intruding?"

Zoe knew sometimes her sister and her husband liked alone time, especially when Gabe had been gone for a while. Honeymoon time, her mother called it, though they'd been married for years.

"Not at all. In fact—" Chloe lowered her voice slightly "—you'd be doing me a favor. Things are a little tense around here right now."

"Oh?"

Chloe and Gabe had a passionate relationship. Sometimes too much so, especially when they fought. It didn't happen often, but when they did fight, it could really be strained around their place.

"I'm not sure I want to be a buffer," she said.

"It's not that bad. Come on over."

Zoe went. It beat sitting around her apartment wondering about Cal.

Gabe greeted her at the door with a kiss on the cheek.

"Congratulations are in order, I hear. But secretly," he said as he ushered her into the spacious flat.

Chloe gave her a hug and looked rueful.

"I told. I tell Gabe everything."

"It's okay. I'm wondering if I'm going about this wrong. Maybe we should have made sure I could get pregnant before doing anything. Though Cal wanted it legal and all."

"Where is he? He would be welcomed here as well," Gabe said.

"Business in Europe," Zoe replied vaguely.

She knew from years of experience not to say anything that could be used as intel by others. Even family. Not that she worried about anyone in her family, but as Cal had emphasized time and again, no one knew completely who was listening.

"See, it's a way of life for our generation," Gabe said to Chloe.

"What is?" Zoe asked, shedding her jacket and laying it across one of the chairs.

"That couples are too busy flying around the world to settle down and start a family," Chloe said.

"Huh?"

"I mentioned considering a baby and he about exploded," she said.

"I did not. Merely that our lifestyle isn't suitable for children. I'm gone half the month on average and you work all kinds of hours."

"I need to show clients the homes when best for them," Chloe said defensively.

"I'm not complaining, love, just saying."

Zoe moved into the lounge area and sat on one of the modern chairs. She enjoyed visiting her sister's flat because the furnishings were so different from her own more traditional pieces. Despite a minimalistic look, the place was welcoming and comfortable.

"So you think I'm crazy to try for a baby?" she asked Gabe.

"Not at all. Your hours are regular, you know where you'll be and when. Routine is best for a baby. Not for us, though."

Zoe looked at her sister. She could see the annoyance behind the smile she gave. The two of them were too close for her to be fooled. Chloe was upset her husband didn't agree with her.

"So," Zoe said, hoping some topic would pop into mind to get away from this one. Otherwise, she was leaving.

"Where did you just come back from, Gabe?"

"Brussels. Is that where Cal is?"

"Why, is something going down over there?" she countered.

She didn't want to admit she herself didn't even know where her boss was.

"This and that," he replied. "I'll start the grill."

He walked out onto their terrace. It was too cold to sit outside without getting bundled up, but Gabe liked grilling in all weather, and he was only outside a short time to check the meat.

"What's that all about?" Zoe asked when the door closed behind him.

"Nothing specific. We've been arguing more lately. We agreed no children when we married, but I mentioned your quest and said we might consider reevaluating our original position and he about exploded. Don't worry, it'll blow over. And you don't know you can't get pregnant. Give yourself a chance. You just started. Some people take months once they are ready to conceive."

"And some never do."

She had to keep that thought in the forefront. There were no guarantees.

"Especially if the prospective father's in Europe and I have no idea when he's coming back."

"Don't you think of Cal as your husband?" Chloe asked.

She brought a tray of cold drinks from the open bar. Setting them on the glass coffee table, she sat on the sofa.

Zoe looked at her. She forgot the story she'd told her sister.

"We've been working together for so long, I think of him more like a colleague."

Pathetically weak. Would her sister buy it?

Zoe sipped one of the cold cola beverages and changed the subject.

"Did you hear Sean is dating a vet?"

"Military or animal?" Chloe asked.

"Veterinarian. Large animal vet, from what Bridget told me when she called last night."

Bridget was a younger sister who had been to dinner at their parents' home Wednesday and gathered all the gossip about brothers and sisters—especially brothers.

"Since when?" Chloe asked.

"A few weeks. Probably not serious, but can you picture our debonair brother dating anyone who gets yucky helping birth calves?"

Chloe laughed and shook her head. She asked other questions and the topic of babies was left behind.

Zoe had a pleasant evening with her sister and brother-in-law, talking about current events, speculating on Sean's new girlfriend and catching up. She was pleasantly tired when she returned home. If she and Cal were married—conventionally that was—they would have evenings like that, visiting family and friends. Laughing, enjoying good food and sharing part of their lives.

Did Cal have a circle of friends he spent time with? She knew about his friend Jason, and the various women he'd dated over the years. Maybe he preferred clubbing to visiting at friends' homes. Or even solitary pursuits like sailing.

Her idea of quiet family evenings could be totally foreign to him. Would he fit in with her family if they had a baby?

By late the following week Zoe was getting concerned. Emily said she heard from Cal a time or two, not to worry. He'd return when it was time.

Only Emily wasn't watching a calendar for auspicious days to conceive. Zoe was. And the days were ticking by.

Thursday shortly after lunch, Zoe got a call from Cal.

"Where are you?" she asked.

"In my office. Come in, will you?"

"I'll be right there."

Emily was not at her desk, so Zoe knocked on the door which was slightly ajar.

Cal opened it. He looked tired, rumpled and wonderful. How could she have forgotten in the short time he'd been gone how wildly handsome he was? His dark eyes gleamed when they looked at her.

"Welcome back," she said as he pulled her gently into the office and shut the door.

"I'm amazingly glad to be back," he said, and pulled her into his arms to kiss her.

The folders slid to the floor, the papers whooshing out and going every which way. But neither noticed. His arms held her tightly. Her mouth met his for the kiss and she responded with enthusiasm. All caution flew out of her mind. She'd missed him, and he was home safe.

The embrace continued with Cal holding her like he'd never let her go. Finally he pulled back a little to look at her.

"I'm tired, out of sorts and have a meeting with the White House in a couple of hours. But I wanted to see you first. How are we doing timewise?"

"It's smack in the middle," she said breathlessly.

"Then let's not waste a minute more," he said, beginning to trail kisses along her cheek, jaw, throat.

His hands caressed, his lips inflamed. She couldn't get close enough. When he shrugged out of his jacket, she helped. He unfastened her blouse, she unbuttoned his shirt. In no time Cal moved and swept his arm across his desk, dashing everything to the floor.

"Not a bed, but it'll do," he said hoarsely.

Zoe took a breath. It was the most wildly exciting gesture she'd ever seen. This man couldn't wait. Nor could she. She reached for him and leaned back against the cool wood of the desk. Her last thought was she hoped he'd locked the office door.

Zoe dressed in record time, not looking at Cal. They were crazy! What if Emily had entered? What if another staff member had knocked to see if Cal were available? It wouldn't take long for the word to spread that he was back. She scrambled for one shoe.

He had an appointment at the White House soon, for heaven's sake. What had he been thinking?

She reached for her shoe and was dumbfounded by the heap of folders, papers and phone messages on the floor.

Mingling in were pens, pencils and his phone.

"Oh, my word. We've got to get this cleaned up before anyone else shows up!"

He knotted his tie and shrugged.

"Let Emily do it."

Zoe straightened and glared at him.

"We most certainly will not! I don't want the entire world to know what we did. I can't believe it myself. We need to get back in some kind of order before she opens that door."

"She's taking a late lunch."

His eyes held amusement as he watched Zoe begin to frantically gather hands full of papers, stuffing them in folders and stacking them on his desk.

"Some of those papers there belong in the Sorenson folder," he said as he knotted his tie.

"Then get them," she said, scrambling to gather other sheets. She placed the phone on his desk, moved it slightly and then patted it as if willing it to remain in place.

Cal watched bemused. She was going to have the office suspiciously clean if he didn't stop her.

But he was enjoying the show. Every time she leaned over, her skirt molded her shapely bottom. Her feet were still without shoes, the shimmer of her stockings catching the light. Her hair was disheveled, any lipstick long gone.

He felt a kick in the gut. He'd purposefully kept all thoughts of Zoe at bay while in Europe. He'd needed all his concentration for the job at hand. And he was due to debrief the president in less than an hour. He had to get home, shower, change and make it to the White House in less than sixty minutes.

But he couldn't move. He was fascinated as she muttered

to herself all the while she snatched up papers and stuffed them randomly into waiting folders. He'd have a mess to clean up. But the overpowering desire that had swept through him when she came in had been unexpected.

He'd acted totally out of character. Never before had he made love to someone on a desktop. The window to conceive was not that great to begin with. He'd been gone for days, keeping a hectic pace that never relaxed. As soon as he finished with the president, he planned to sack out for at least twelve hours.

At least he tried to justify the situation.

If he knew Zoe, she hadn't moved into his place while he'd been gone. Were they back to square one now?

"Where are you staying these days?" he asked as he finished tying his shoes.

"At home, where else?"

"My place."

The desk began to resemble the way he usually kept it. It'd pass muster with Emily at least. He waited for her to elaborate. She remained silent.

"I thought you were moving into my flat," he said finally.

"The more I considered it, the more I didn't like the idea. The current arrangement suits me."

"The beach cottage or the desk?" he said whimsically.

"The beach cottage. This was an aberration. Do you realize anyone could have walked in on us?"

When her voice rose slightly at the end he realized she was really upset by the aftermath.

Instead of a warm memory, he'd embarrassed her.

"It wasn't my intention. I'd love to discuss this with you, but really I have to go. Later?" he asked, checking his wristwatch again.

"No, not later. Maybe not ever."

She jammed her foot into her shoe and stormed to the door.

Just as she reached for the knob, Cal reached out and stopped her, turning her to face him.

"You could have said to stop at any time," he said quietly.

"I didn't want to," she said petulantly.

He threw back his head and roared with laughter. A moment later, he leaned over and brushed his lips against her cheek.

"I'll remember that, not the histrionics about the mess we made. I'll call you when I'm finished at the White House."

"Don't bother. I'll be busy."

She pulled her arm free and twisted the lock and threw open the door, almost running down the hall.

Cal watched until she disappeared into the ladies' room.

"That went well," he murmured as he headed out.

He ran his fingers through his hair. He'd acted like a love-struck teenager, unable to finesse the feelings he had when around Zoe. There was no excuse, except she had been more than willing. He could remember the sounds she'd made urging him on. The sweet touch of her hands on his skin. Her mouth kissing him like there was no tomorrow.

Blast it, he didn't need this fresh memory. He had a debriefing to attend.

Chapter Nine

Zoe washed her face, dried it with paper towels and finger combed her hair. She looked at herself in the mirror. She'd tell people she was feverish if anyone saw her between here and her car. Trying to act calm, she walked from the rest room to her office, gathered her purse and jacket and fled. The few people she passed in the hallway were too intent on their own concerns to speculate about her.

She drove to her apartment. It was midafternoon on a Thursday. She never left work early unless she was seriously incapacitated. What did she do now?

The flush of pleasure that swept through her when she remembered Cal impatiently sweeping the folders off his desk caught her by surprise. Okay, analyze it. She liked it. She more than liked it.

And she was amazed he'd ever do such a thing. It didn't fit with her image of the hard-edged security man.

But then it hadn't fit her own image. She wasn't the kind of woman to have wild sex on an office desk. She couldn't believe it.

She took a quick shower, changed into warm slacks and a sweater and began cleaning her apartment. Good therapy, plus she wanted it to look nice if Cal came by after his debriefing.

By seven she had to concede he wasn't coming.

It was after ten and Zoe was in bed when the phone rang. She knew who was calling.

"Hello?"

"We just finished. It's too late to come over and I'm beat. Want to go to the beach this weekend?" Cal said.

She could hear the background noise of the street.

"You've been there for a long time."

"It's not my crisis, Protection, Inc. got involved peripherally. But once the president heard of the situation, he called in some experts. I had to go over everything more than once. They don't like it, but that doesn't change the facts."

"About?"

He sighed.

"I'm so tired I forgot. Let's say a minor glitch in Brussels and leave it at that."

"How about we go to your place in Richmond, this weekend. That would be more practical."

"And you are a practical woman, right?"

"Yes."

"Think of me before you go to sleep," he said and hung up.

As if she'd think of anything else.

Emily called Zoe the next morning right after she arrived at work.

"Cal wants to know if you are available to attend the concert at Kennedy Center tonight. He has season tickets and finds he can attend tonight's performance. It's the music of John Williams. He said if you can go, he'll pick you up at seven and to plan to have a late supper afterward."

"Tell Cal thanks. I'll be ready."

Zoe loved attending performances at the Kennedy Center. It gave her a chance to dress up. Since Cal rarely saw her outside of the office in the past, everything she had would be new to him. Too bad. She'd have loved an excuse to splurge on a new dress. Still, she was saving her money for her precious baby. Even a night at Kennedy Center wouldn't sway her.

Cal knocked on her apartment door promptly at seven.

"You look lovely," he said when she opened the door.

Zoe wore a long burgundy velvet dress, with a high collar. She'd arranged her hair swept up and pinned with glittering combs. A bit more makeup than she normally wore complemented the deep color of her gown. She felt stylish and feminine with the glittering jewelry that complemented the outfit.

"Thank you."

She was pleased he thought so. She might not be able to compete with his model-gorgeous girlfriends, but she did dress up nicely.

"Sorry for the short notice. I have season tickets and often give them to employees or clients, but had saved these for tonight. I like his work. If I had been home from Europe earlier, I'd have invited you earlier," he said.

"I had no other plans, so this is a special treat."

A date. They had made love several times, been married a month and she counted this as their first real date.

Did Cal realize that? They'd had several meals together, but he and various staff members often had meals together when discussing business. Those didn't count.

She even felt as shy as a first date.

"Ready?"

She handed him her coat and he helped her put it on. In moments they were speeding toward the glittering Kennedy Center. Lighted at night it looked like a huge confection, its reflection doubling in the Potomac River. Columns marched around the building. Despite its huge size, it looked light and magical with all the illumination.

Valet parking took care of the car. Zoe loved mingling with the others who had come to hear the music. Glitter and dazzling displays of jewelry had her gazing around in awe. Conversations ebbed and flowed, laughter rang out.

"It's always the same, yet unexpected and wondrous," she said, holding Cal's arm. "I love coming here."

"You'll have to let me know what you want to see and I'll keep those tickets," he said as they moved through the groups chatting and greeting acquaintances.

Cal spoke to a couple on his right, introducing Zoe to the McGillroys. He nodded to a beautiful woman with one of the junior congressmen from Wisconsin. Zoe wondered if she was one he used to date. She fit the profile—slender, beautiful and exquisitely attired. The dress Zoe had been so happy with now seemed conservative in comparison.

"A bit too much skin for the Kennedy Center, I'd say," he murmured when they were past.

"I thought men liked to see skin."

He glanced at her.

"On the right woman and at the right time."

She couldn't have written anything more perfect to say.

The music was wonderful. She enjoyed the entire

program. Cal had been attentive, holding her hand during much of the performance. Which, given all they'd done together, shouldn't have been the big deal it was.

Zoe could hardly listen to the music. Her entire body was tingling from that connection. Her senses swam with awareness and desire. She wanted to drive back to his place and make love all night.

After the show, he drove to a small restaurant near the Mall. It was dark and intimate. Zoe was charmed he'd thought of it for their late dinner.

The maître d' seated them in a small alcove, with enough light to read the menu, yet with a definite romantic overtone. She glanced at Cal. The man constantly surprised her. She never thought of him as being romantic.

"This is lovely," she said.

He nodded, reading the menu.

"A friend recommended it. It could do with a bit more light."

So much for romance, she thought with a wry sigh.

After they ordered, Zoe sipped her iced water. She wasn't drinking wine tonight—not until after the baby came—if she should be so lucky.

What to talk about? Not work. Nor their odd relationship. Did she and Cal have anything else in common?

"I need your help," he said.

"Oh?"

"The house Uncle Hal and I lived in was built in the 1920s. He upgraded it when he bought it but that was thirty years ago. I'm not much into that kind of thing. I like the way your apartment feels, so can you do something with the house before I try to rent it out? I thought we could go room by room when we're there, deciding what needed to be done. I'll make sure the electricity and plumbing is up-to-date, but I draw the line at figuring out paint colors."

"I'd be happy to."

Cal nodded. That was taken care of. He'd hoped she'd agree. He knew to build a team, people had to share a common goal. He'd thought about it a lot in his downtime in Europe. He and Zoe weren't a team yet, though they did share one common goal. But he wanted more. A project they both could work on would do the trick—at least he hoped so.

"It'll probably take a while," he cautioned.

"I hope we can do it in a few weeks. You don't want the house to remain vacant too long, at least that's what Chloe is always saying. We can scope out the project this weekend, make a time schedule, list items to have repaired or replaced. Did you want to do the work yourself or hire someone?"

"Do it myself?"

Cal hadn't thought about that. He remembered hot summer days when he and Uncle Hal had painted the entire downstairs. The walls hadn't been touched since, if he remembered correctly.

She watched him. Did she think he couldn't do it?

"You'd help, too?" he asked.

"Sure. I could get Chloe and Gabe to join in, I bet. If you really want things done fast, we could invite the entire Blackstone family down one weekend. With thirteen of us working, fourteen counting you, we'd sweep through in a day."

"Let's start out with you and me."

The plan was to build something together, not whip through the project.

"Besides, I thought you weren't going to tell anyone about our marriage."

"I wouldn't have to tell them anything about that, only say a friend needed help."

"We'll see."

She laughed.

"You'll make a perfect father. That's what my folks say when they are stalling and will eventually say no."

He liked the sparkle in her eyes and the sound of her laughter. It surprised him when she grew serious a moment later.

"It doesn't bother you, keeping our marriage secret, does it? It's not that I'm ashamed of it or anything."

He shook his head.

"I understand you don't want aftereffects if we don't succeed. It's fine, Zoe. Don't worry about me."

She bit her lip and gave a halfhearted nod.

"It's hard not to," she said.

What did she mean by that? He was used to taking care of himself. If anyone needed to be worried about it was her. He hadn't liked the up-close impact of the pain she experienced each month. He hoped she could get pregnant soon.

The waiter brought their meal and as they began to eat, they discussed plans for the house.

When Cal reached Zoe's apartment, he found a parking place and withdrew a small bag from the trunk before opening her door.

She eyed the suitcase and then looked at him.

"Staying over?"

"This is the time, right?"

He'd packed before he left home, knowing they'd be together for the next few nights. All the more reason for them to move in together. Since she hadn't acted on the suggestion, he suspected it would be a harder sell than he'd originally envisioned.

At least they'd have the weekend together. Maybe she'd see the advantages as the days passed.

With his remark, the joy of the evening vanished for Zoe. It *was* the right time. Only, tonight had been so special. She liked feeling she'd been invited for the pleasure of her company. She'd enjoyed the music, the discussion at the restaurant and even the plans they'd made for the renovation project.

Now she felt like a laboratory test subject—make sure to procreate on this day.

"You don't wish me to stay?" he asked as they rode the elevator.

"Of course. As you said, this is the right time."

She questioned the wisdom of this scheme. There was more to it than she'd anticipated. The more she was around Cal, the more she liked it. She'd been thrilled when she'd seen him yesterday after his trip. Disappointed when he hadn't come to see her last night. Happy about tonight—until now.

Yet here he was and she still wasn't satisfied. What was wrong with her?

"Only?" he asked.

"Only nothing," she said, her gaze fixed on the brushed metal doors of the elevator. "I'm being silly."

"As in?" he probed.

"As in nothing, Cal. Leave it, okay?"

She couldn't explain. He'd think she was nuts and probably wouldn't want a crazy woman to be the mother of his baby.

Once the initial awkwardness was passed and they began to make love, Zoe forgot all her objections. She loved being touched by Cal. His kisses drove her to the stars. And when they joined together she knew it was as close to heaven as she was going to get on earth.

All thoughts of clinical laboratory work fled. She loved this man. She'd treasure every moment spent with him and if they were lucky enough to have a baby, she'd rejoice all her life.

If not, she'd have to let him go. It wasn't fair to him to keep him from having a family of his own. She had brothers and sisters, nieces and nephews and could make a place for herself as favorite aunt. Cal had no one.

The thought brought a pang. She wished instead of making this arrangement, he'd genuinely fallen for her as she had for him.

Reaching out to link her hand with his, she snuggled closer. Nothing lasted forever. She'd take what she could get and cherish every moment. If he walked away and she had the operation with no baby between them, she'd still remember these nights and how for a short time she felt as if she were the most important woman in the world for Jedidiah Callahan.

The day was sunny and warm as they drove to Richmond. Zoe called Chloe to let her know she'd be gone for the weekend. The drive along the parkway wasn't as pretty in early

November with the trees denuded of leaves. She'd like to drive down in the summer and see the difference.

"Did you visit your uncle often?" she asked as the miles sped by.

"Not often enough. He'd come up to Washington from time to time. He liked going to RFK Stadium to watch baseball. Didn't come up as much in the winter. Too cold, he said."

"It does feel cold with the damp air from the river," she said.

"Richmond gets snow, so he had it cold. But he liked being home."

"He was an accountant, you said?"

"Yes, worked for thirty some years for a meat packing firm. He took early retirement a year or so ago. We talked about renting a big cruiser and exploring the Chesapeake Bay. Even talked about going out on to the Atlantic. I wish now that I'd pushed for a firm date and done it."

"He wasn't very old—you couldn't know he'd die when he did," she said.

"Still, regrets for things not done don't fade easily."

Which was the entire reason she was trying for a baby. If she couldn't have one, she'd be heartbroken. But at least she'd know all her life she'd done what she could. That was one regret she wouldn't have.

"Thank you, Cal. You're making sure I don't have regrets for things not done."

"Hang in there, Zoe. We'll have that baby."

They arrived at the house late morning. It had a definitely deserted look about it. There were leaves that needed raking and bushes that needed pruning. The house itself looked empty, as if the life had gone out of it when Hal died. The windows were blank. The paint looked tired.

"You planning to paint the outside as well?" Zoe asked.

Cal climbed out of the car and studied the facade.

"It looks lik it needs it. Now isn't the best time of year, however. Maybe come spring. Let's go inside and make plans."

Zoe was glad to have something to do. She knew they needed to stick close for the next couple of days. She appreciated having the project to focus on. Otherwise she'd think of nothing but Cal.

And she dare not let him suspect how she felt.

Zoe grew more excited as they progressed through the house. Cal was serious about relying on her to design the color schemes and make suggestions to bring the house up-to-date. She could almost pretend they were planning their first place together. She'd give each room an assessment, then think aloud of what could be done. He'd agree, she'd jot notes and they moved on to the next.

By dinnertime she had a tablet full of notes and ideas.

"I'd like to get this in some better order, maybe combine the different needs from each room so we'd only have to have a plumber or electrician out once and have them take care of everything, rather than call back and forth as we get to each room," Zoe said, bubbling with ideas and wanting to get schedules drawn up.

"You're in charge," he said, leaning back in the comfy sofa in the living room.

Cal had ordered pizza, preferring that to having to cook.

Zoe felt energized. "This will be a lovely home when you're finished."

"When we're finished," he said, closing his eyes.

"Are you going to sleep?"

"Not yet," he said. "I'm envisioning how the place will look."

"I bet a young family would love this home. The backyard is huge. Think of the fun the children could have. Did you have a fort and a tree house?"

"I had a tree house, Jason had the fort. And there's a trail down to a stream. We had some major naval battles on that creek," Cal said.

Zoe tried to picture a younger Cal playing with his friend. She and her brothers had done their share of battles in makeshift plains of the sand at the beach. They used to make small homes and forts from wooden matches and end up burning them as a grand finale of each battle. Would her baby be part of the next generation at the beach?

"My brothers liked battles," she said.

She still couldn't picture Cal as a boy.

"Do you have any photos from when you were a child?"

She'd seen a couple of him in pictures of his uncle after the funeral. Had there been more?

"There're likely to be around somewhere," he said vaguely.

Glancing around, he narrowed his eyes.

"I suppose the best plan would be to do one room at a time. Decide what's to be done, clear it out, get it painted, repaired as needed and move on."

"If you came every weekend, you could finish in a couple

of months," she said, jotting some more notes.

"I do have a company to run," he said.

"Delegate."

She looked over at him and met his gaze.

He stared at her for a moment. "Maybe." He closed his eyes again.

Zoe was happy to doodle on her paper, capturing different tasks and listing the order she'd prioritize things.

"We need to get a hotel room," Cal said a few moments later.

He'd been thinking about taking Zoe to bed ever since they sat down. It was for the sake of the baby, he told himself. He lied. He wanted her.

"A hotel? I thought we'd stay here," Zoe said.

"There's only a single bed in my old room. The guest room's bed is equally small as you know from your last visit. And I don't feel right about using Uncle Hal's."

She nodded.

"That makes sense. But we can't stay at a hotel every time we come, that would be silly when you own this house. Maybe you should get a bigger bed in your room."

"You won't be coming every time. Just when we need to try for the baby," he said.

She went still. He opened his eyes and looked at her. She was staring at the list she'd just made.

"You're right—what was I thinking," she said in a quiet voice.

Had he said something wrong?

"You can come if you want," he said.

Her smile looked phony and she wouldn't look at him.

"Don't be silly. This is your family home. I'll get the list of tasks printed out and give it to you. I'll have lots to do on other weekends. No time to come down every week."

She carefully wrote another line on her tablet.

Cal wished he knew what was going through her mind. Did she actually want to come with him? The sooner he got the house fixed up, the sooner he could rent it out and have one less thing to worry about.

Could Zoe already be pregnant? Once they knew for sure, would the nights together stop? Cal studied her as she kept her gaze on the tablet. He'd never had such a close relationship with another woman. He'd never lived with anyone but his uncle. Never considered moving in together with any women he'd dated. They'd been dates, not possible mates.

He was startled. Was he thinking of Zoe as a possible mate?

If she became pregnant, if she had his child, he was willing to make a family unit—for the sake of the child.

Or was it also for his sake? He hadn't spent a lot of time with Uncle Hal in the years after he graduated from high school. First there was the army, then college, getting Protection, Inc, started. Would he do better with a family of his own?

Try as he might, he couldn't picture himself as a father. Did that foreshadow the future? He didn't want to think so. To make up for the lost baby, he wanted to be the best father possible to this child. He wished he could have held his baby. Told it just once he loved it.

Zoe rose and, holding the tablet like a shield, headed out

of the room.

"I want to check on something," she said.

Something was definitely wrong. He hated it when women wouldn't talk about a problem. How could he fix things if he didn't know what was wrong in her world?

Zoe walked through the kitchen and out onto the back porch. It was dark already, and growing colder. She didn't care. Blinking hard, she kept back tears. Cal couldn't have said anything more blatant to remind her theirs was an arrangement to have a baby, not a relationship. He wasn't growing to love her. She was living in a fool's paradise if she hoped for a happy-ever-after ending. Life didn't work that way.

Taking a deep breath, she tried to think. But mostly she focused on the hurt she felt with his words. She was nothing more than a container for him to fill with a baby. When it wasn't the right time, thank you, he'd do fine without her.

She'd brought it on herself. Now she wondered if the cost was too high. How would they live through the years ahead if he merely came by because of the child? Would they divorce and he find someone else?

That she'd find someone else seemed unlikely. She hadn't found the right man in all her twenty-eight years—until now. And it seemed he still wasn't the right one.

She wanted to go home. She was not going to give in to Cal's suggestion that they move in together. In fact, she was going to reevaluate her entire plan. If she wasn't pregnant by the time her next period was due, she was going to decide whether to continue or not.

The thought of not trying brought a pang. Yet so did the idea of falling more and more in love with a man who couldn't even have her tag along when he fixed up his uncle's home unless it was the right time of the month.

"Zoe, what's wrong?" he asked behind her.

"Nothing, I was thinking about a summer garden."

She refused to let him know how hurt she felt.

"It's pitch-dark, you can't see anything."

"I remember what the yard looks like. I can sketch from memory."

"Then you don't need to be out in the cold."

She drew in another breath, feeling steadier than before. The threat of tears were gone. She'd make it through the weekend. Turning, she walked toward Cal.

"You're right, I'm through being out in the cold. Let's find that hotel. I'm tired."

There was an available room at a nearby hotel. But tonight Zoe wasn't thinking about making a baby. She was making memories to last her during the years to come when she opened her arms to Cal.

Chapter Ten

Two weeks later Zoe woke feeling achy. She had avoided Cal as much as possible without causing comment over the last few days.

True to her word, she'd worked on the project for renovating the Richmond house and by the Thursday after they'd returned from Richmond had presented Cal with a printout of all her notes and recommendations.

When he'd asked her about contacting painters and carpenters, she'd pleaded a heavy workload and asked if Emily could handle that.

She didn't want to invest herself in a project she might not even see to completion.

Today, that seemed wise. Feeling slightly depressed, she rose and debated going to work. Her period was scheduled to start tomorrow and she already felt some of the cramping that was sure to accompany it.

She was not pregnant.

And she wasn't going to continue in the futile effort.

Her doctor had told her it might prove difficult if not impossible to conceive. Why not give in to the inevitable and schedule the operation? The pain caused incapacity each month wasn't going to go away. It could get worse.

She needed to tell Cal. Zoe knew he 'd try to talk her out of it. He was tenacious in his pursuit of objectives—at least at work. And she knew he grieved at the loss of the other baby.

He needed a woman who could give him lots of love and lots of children. She only counted in one aspect.

He'd put up a fuss, but this was the wise decision. He never stayed with any woman long, so before she knew it, he'd find someone else. Maybe to have a family with or maybe to squire around to social events as he'd been doing all the years she'd known him.

At least no one else but Chloe and Gabe knew the full story. She must have known deep inside that it would end this way. That's why she'd been so insistent no one knew about the marriage or the baby quest.

Once the marriage ended, they'd go on as they had before. Or if it became too painful to see him with another woman, Zoe knew she could find a job with another security firm.

Only, deep down she didn't want to change a thing. She wanted to share a child with Cal, watch it grow, develop. See her parents as doting grandparents, her sisters and brothers as extended family the child would love through the years. Have their son or daughter play with cousins, share in family holidays and birthdays. And spend summers in carefree fun at the seashore. And she wanted Cal with her every step of the way.

By the time she finished her hot chocolate, her mind was made up. She was calling in the vacation time she was owed. She'd go to the sea. Any comfort would be found there.

Calling Chloe, she told her where she was going.

"Honestly, girl, you go there more in winter than summer," her twin said.

"Best time, quiet, no people around. Beside, I want to be by myself for a while."

"Burning the candle at both ends?"

"No. Some thinking to do."

"About?" Chloe sounded cautious.

"About ending this farce of a marriage and scheduling the operation."

"What are you talking about? You have hardly given yourself a fair chance at getting pregnant."

"It's complicated."

Chloe was quiet for a moment.

"You've fallen for Cal, haven't you? He's so blind. Tell him."

"That is the last thing he wants. He only agreed to help me because I wanted it so much."

And because of his lost baby and his uncle's death. But Zoe wasn't sharing Cal's private business even with her sister.

"I'll go with you."

"I don't need handholding."

Then suddenly she wanted her sister to go. Maybe talking things through would help.

"Pick me up when you leave," Chloe said.

"Around ten," Zoe said.

For the first time since she'd made her decision, she felt like the future might not be impossible to live through.

She packed a few things. Called the office to let her supervisor know she was taking off for a few days. She debated not calling Cal, but remembered the last time she'd tried to dodge him.

He answered after one ring.

"Callahan."

"Cal." Zoe kept her tone light though her throat ached with tears. "I'm taking off for a few days. Chloe and I are heading for the beach—where else?"

"Anything wrong?"

"No." She took a breath. "Just some girl time. I'll call you when I get back."

"I'm glad you called. I have a last minute meeting scheduled in San Francisco. I'll be gone for a couple of days but back by Sunday. I'll come by your place on my way home."

She started to argue, but didn't.

"Fine."

He'd find out Sunday night that she wasn't home. And he'd be too tired after his trip to hunt her up at the cottage.

"Have a good trip, new business, I hope and not a crisis."

"New business."

Cal often presented the strategy for security to new clients, depending on the complexity of the assignment.

"Always good to hear. Have a great flight."

She hung up and burst into tears. She hated the way her life was going.

"It's freezing here," Chloe said, opening the door to the cottage shortly after lunch. They'd stopped in Waterford for a quick meal. After which they paid a brief visit to the local grocery store.

"The heater works fine. There's nothing better than curling up in one of grandma's old quilts on the porch and letting the cold breeze try to get to you," Zoe said as she deposited her bags of food on the counter.

"Yes, there is—warm summer evenings with a balmy breeze to cool you down and a crab feed in progress."

Chloe put her own grocery bag down and rubbed her

hands together while Zoe went to turn on the furnace.

"You're such a fair weather gal," she said.

"You bet."

"I appreciate Gabe being okay for you to come for a few days."

"That's the third time you've said that. He was fine with it."

Zoe glanced at her sister. Was there something in her tone? Maybe she was annoying her with her gratitude, but she did appreciate it. Not every husband was happy to have his wife take off for several days on a moment's notice.

"Let's get this place warm and start dinner. I love the smell of spaghetti sauce simmering all day," Chloe said, already putting away the supplies they'd purchased.

Soon it was warm enough to take off their coats. Once settled in, they began to make their grandmother's sauce. The pot was soon giving off tantalizing aromas.

"So tell me all," Chloe said as she settled in one of the comfortable chairs in the main room.

Zoe sat on the sofa.

"It's a dumb idea. I left it too late. There's no guarantee that I can get pregnant. Dr. Wright tried to tell me that. She was honest when she said it'd be very unlikely."

"But you haven't tried for long. Maybe another couple of months."

"No."

"Because of Cal?"

"Because of how much I am falling in love with him. He's more than the man I thought I knew at the office. Whenever we spend time together, I learn new things and admire him. Plus the physical attraction grows each time we get near each other. I have a hard time keeping from throwing myself at him whenever he's in the same room."

"And he'd object?"

"Duh. We didn't marry for love like you and Gabe. The whole reason we kept quiet was just for this result."

"What do you mean—you planned this from the beginning?" Chloe asked in surprise.

"I didn't plan it precisely, but I think deep inside I knew it'd end like this. I didn't want people blaming him for our divorce, so if no one knew we were married, no one could."

"Does he want a divorce?"

"I'm not keeping a man tied to me when we can't have children. That's not fair."

"Adopt."

Zoe shrugged.

"Maybe, someday. But I can do that on my own. I don't need Cal for that. And he deserves his own kids. He's the last of his family since his uncle died. Don't you think he wants his own flesh and blood?"

"I'm surprised he wants kids at all. Gabe doesn't," Chloe said.

"You didn't either. Have you changed your mind?"

"Not really. I don't know. Your solution has me thinking. What if I did change my mind? Maybe I have what you have and can't get pregnant."

"No, you'd know it. And if you start getting symptoms, you'd have time to act. I left it too late. Still, I like my job. I love my nieces and nephews. I can make that work."

"Don't give up yet."

Zoe looked at Chloe.

"I have to."

Cal arrived back in Washington at five o'clock on Sunday afternoon. The presentation had gone well, even though it'd been so rushed. Not a crisis on the part of Protection, Inc., but certainly one on the side of his new client. He was satisfied the company could handle the situation without a problem.

He drove to Zoe's apartment. He thought about calling her, but didn't know what she and her sister might be doing. He was surprised at how much he wanted to see her.

Knocking on her door a little later he waited impatiently for her to open. Maybe he should have brought some flowers or something.

The thought knocked him for a loop. What was this, some kind of courtship? They were already married. And trying for a baby. He didn't need to bring flowers to see her. Though maybe he'd suggest they go out to eat. No sense in her preparing a meal for two on short notice.

There was no bright welcome. There was no sound from her apartment at all.

He knocked again. Waited.

Flipping open his phone, he dialed her cell.

"Zoe's phone," Chloe said.

"Is she there? This is Cal."

"She's in bed, cramps."

"Oh."

He leaned against the wall. A wave of disappointment swept through him. He'd hoped she'd become pregnant. Why was it if a man wasn't careful, one slip could end up with a baby. Yet they'd been trying for weeks and nothing.

"How's she doing?" he asked.

"Not as bad as some times. I'll tell her you called when she wakes up."

"I'll come out."

"Don't. She's not feeling up to it and I don't want to have to entertain you and take care of her at the same time."

"You don't have to do either. I can take care of my wife."

"We're doing fine here, Cal. She'll call you."

With that, Chloe hung up.

He jammed the phone in his pocket and walked down the hall. He'd head for the cottage first thing in the morning. Chloe didn't call the shots in his marriage.

Shortly after nine, Cal received a call from Zoe.

"How are you feeling?" he asked.

"Better. Chloe fixed me some clam chowder. It's so good, with crackers. She said you called. How did your trip go?"

"Fine. I'm coming there in the morning."

"I was afraid of that, so I called tonight. Don't come, Cal."

"What's going on, Zoe?"

"Nothing. Everything. I don't know, but I'm not pregnant, and am too tired to fight the inevitable any longer."

He felt a sick dread.

"What does that mean?"

"I'm calling my doctor in the morning and scheduling a time to see her to give her the okay to schedule the operation."

"We haven't had our baby yet," he said. "You can't stop after only trying for such a short time."

"I need to…this is not getting better."

"Chloe said this time wasn't as bad as some of the others."

"Some times are barely noticeable, others I can scarcely live through the pain. None of it's going to get better. This way you can get on with your life and I can get on with mine."

"How do you mean?"

"A quick divorce, no one the wiser. We don't even have

to tell anyone ever."

"That's it? Hide it away pretend it never happened? We are married."

"Only because that's your condition to this entire situation. I was willing to try without that legal tie. Now we break it."

"What if I don't want to break it?"

"Cal."

He wasn't sure if he heard a sound. There was a pause, then Zoe spoke again.

"You'll find someone who can give you dozens of babies. Only make sure you get married first, no more Suzannes."

"I tried that this go round."

"I know. I'm sorry." She disconnected.

Cal put on warm clothes, packed a couple of things and headed out. He wasn't going to sever ties with Zoe on a weekend she was feeling down because of cramps. They'd hardly tried. He wanted more.

He wanted Zoe.

The entire town of Seagrass Point was dark. No lights shone anywhere. The cottage was in darkness as well. But he could still find his way. He walked up the path to the door and knocked. Then pounded. If both were asleep, they'd need more than a gentle knock.

Chloe flicked on the porch light as she opened the door.

For a moment she stared at him.

"I never thought you'd come. She said she told you it was over."

"It's not over."

Cal stepped inside to convince his wife of that very fact.

"That's the last of the blood work. We'll get the tests

results and move right along," Dr. Wright said. "I've got the OR scheduled for next Tuesday. I know it's a hard decision, but the relief from the pain will be well worth it."

Zoe nodded. She was afraid to speak for fear she'd start crying again. She'd cried more in the last week than any time before in her entire life.

Cal had tried to talk her into giving them a few more months. She'd been steadfast in refusing. Chloe even suggested another month or two might bring Cal around to caring for her.

Zoe didn't believe anything would change. Cal almost broke her heart when he showed up in the middle of the night at the cottage. He'd been very persuasive, in an analytical, logical way. She should have appreciated it more than she had. Normally she loved analytical, logical presentations.

If he'd only said one word of something personal. Anything to give her a hint she meant more to him on a personal level and not some surrogate mother for his child. But he hadn't. She couldn't have expected him to do so. He'd been clear on the terms, as had she at the onset. It wasn't his fault she'd fallen in love with him.

When she left the doctor's office, she almost bumped into Cal.

He took her arm and walked her through the vast lobby of the high-rise building. Once outside, he started left.

"There's a café down here. We can have a cup of coffee and talk."

"Cal, we talked at the cottage. It's all been said. How did you know I was here?"

"Emily found out for me. And I have not said all I need to say."

She could barely keep up with his rapid pace.

"What's the rush?" she asked, glad when he paused by a coffeehouse and held the door for her. Midafternoon wasn't a crowded time. He placed their orders and they took a table near the front windows.

"I'm putting the house in Richmond up for sale," he said.

"You are? Why? I thought you were going to fix it up and then rent it out."

He took a sip of his coffee. If Zoe didn't know better, she'd suspect he was stalling.

"Why?" she repeated.

He looked at her.

"The renovation was my way to do something together— you and me. I don't fit into your world, but I want to. I haven't had much family life ever. It was just me and my uncle. And over the last ten or twelve years, I've been building the business, neglecting my uncle and going along as if life would never change until I was ready."

Zoe could relate to a degree. She had loads of family, and lots of interaction, but she'd focused her life on one area. And now it was too late to do much else but continue to focus on that one area.

"He was proud of you. More than one person mentioned that at the wake," she said.

She studied Cal as he sat beside her. He looked lonely. Could it be? Her heart began to beat faster.

"I thought you were keeping the house," she said softly.

"I said I thought it might bring you and me together."

"We are together."

"No, we're not. We're married—there's a difference."

Zoe nodded. She and Cal certainly didn't have the loving

relationship her sister and her husband shared. If they did, she'd reach out and take his hand, linking with him so he'd know he wasn't alone.

But she kept her fists in her lap, lest she give way.

"So if we're not going to do that together, maybe you'd like to buy a beach cottage."

Zoe blinked at that. "What?"

"You love the one that's in your family. Maybe you'd like to have one of your own, nearby, of course, so you could run back and forth when they're all there. But one that you could go to anytime you wanted."

She wasn't sure she was hearing him correctly.

"You're offering to buy me a cottage?"

"Us."

"Us? Cal, there is no us."

"There could be."

He glanced around impatiently. A group of laughing teenagers entered and the small coffeehouse suddenly seemed overrun.

"Let's get out of here."

Zoe grabbed her cup, glad it was the to-go kind, and almost ran to keep up with him.

Cal didn't speak as they walked toward the Mall. Once on the great expanse, he slowed a little, turned and looked at her.

"I don't want to end our marriage, Zoe."

"Cal, I can't have kids. I was fooling myself, trying one last ditch effort to have a baby. You need a wife who can give you everything you want."

"That's you." He cupped her face in his palms. "I realized our last weekend together that I like spending time with you.

Whether we're looking at driftwood, planning a project or enjoying a concert. Or just lazing around watching a storm together from the porch. Or, maybe I've known it for longer, and didn't admit it to myself. I thought we could keep going like we had been. I wanted you to move into my place. When I thought about it, it sounded convenient. But the truth is, I like waking up next to you. I want more of that. I enjoy watching you move around the kitchen—it's so womanly, and I've not had much of that in my life. Everything about you fascinates me and enchants me. I want you in my life. And I mean to keep you right in the center."

She started to say something, but he shook his head once.

"Let me finish or I might never get the courage to start again."

Zoe blinked at that. This man was afraid of nothing.

"When Suzanne aborted our child, it crushed something in me. Which bloomed again when you said you'd have a baby with me. But the more I get to know you, the more I share your anguish in not having a child. That's the difference. I share it with you. We can adopt, we can lavish attention on your nephews and nieces, or we can forge a strong life just the two of us. Whatever we want. Only, don't shut me out. Don't walk away."

Zoe couldn't believe her ears, but her eyes conveyed the truth. His honest appeal couldn't be faked.

"Did Chloe tell you?" she asked suspiciously.

"Tell me what?"

"That I love you? That's why I wanted to break things off. Not because I didn't want to spend time with you, but because I thought I'd get so deep in love I'd never get out and then when we didn't have a baby, you'd go on to another woman. That would kill me. I had to fight for myself, and end it before I couldn't ever walk away."

"Then you really don't want a divorce?" he asked.

She threw herself into his arms.

"I love you, Cal. I have forever, I think. I tried so hard to resist my sexy boss, but once you said you wanted to have a baby with me, my resistance melted. I fought a good fight, but the result was a foregone conclusion. I love you. Do you really mean it that you don't want to find a wife who can give you a dozen kids?"

"I only want you, Zoe. You have shown me how a family can be. I hope your family will let me in. But if not, you will always be enough for me. I love you, sweetheart. I want us to have fifty or sixty years together. Just don't walk away."

She waited a heartbeat then burst out, "Are you kidding? I love you. I don't want to leave. And don't worry about my family. They'll all love you to bits. And before you know it you'll be a favorite uncle. We have a birthday almost every other week, and holidays are chaotic with everyone at one place or another. Summers we spend lazy days at the shore with barbecues on the sand."

Zoe clung to him, her happiness bubbling over. For a few bright moments, she forgot they'd never have a baby. That their family would forever be small, just the two of them. But with Cal it would be enough.

"We won't have kids of our own," she said slowly. "Cal, are you very sure? You said you were the last of your family. That will always be the situation. I'm so sorry."

"Hush. You will be my family. If we wish, we'll adopt.

That's really what my uncle did, took me on when he didn't have to. We'll fill a home with children we choose to be ours. And we'll teach them everything about the Callahan and Blackstone families to carry on down the generations. I love you, Zoe, not some yet to be conceived child, not some fantasy future with everything ending happy. We'll face all life's challenges together. Right?"

She nodded, her heart brimming with love.

"The next step is to tell your parents."

"Oh-oh. Let's wait until after the operation, and then suggest we want to get married. We'll let my mother put on a big wedding and we'll be the only ones to know our anniversary date is another."

"Unless Chloe or Gabe spills the beans."

"They won't. I love you, Cal."

"I love you now and forever," he said, kissing her deeply.

Zoe and Cal slipped away to the sea cottage for the weekend. They walked along the shore, making plans for the future. She looked at each dwelling as they passed, considering whether it would be suitable for a home for them, though none were for sale that she knew of. Still, it was fun to dream of a future—with Cal.

"Are you sure you want to sell the Richmond home?" she asked more than once.

"Don't you want a home of your own?" he responded, threading his fingers through hers as they walked.

"The beach cottage has been in our family for generations, we'll be able to use it. So why not have a home in Richmond as well?"

"Because we are more likely to come here than back to

Richmond. Once you've recovered from the operation, we'll start looking for a place. If you don't like my condo, we can buy another primary residence together. But I think here at the shore we will also want a home of our own."

"Suits me. We need one with a porch that faces the sea, so we can sit there during storms."

Cal rearranged his schedule for the next week. He planned to accompany Zoe to the hospital, wait through the operation and then, when she was ready, take her home—to their home—to recover. They had moved a few of her things on Monday, enough to carry her through the first few days. Once she was fully recovered, they'd tell her family.

Tuesday they arrived at the hospital early. Dr. Wright was already there doing rounds. Her nurse contacted her and she hurried into the admissions office.

"Zoe, I tried calling you several times over the last few days."

She looked at Cal.

"Dr. Wright, this is my husband, Jedidiah Callahan. I'm sorry, I wasn't home. I took a weekend away before today and turned my phone off," Zoe said, gripping Cal's hand. "A last mini-vacation before the operation."

"There won't be an operation," Dr. Wright said. "There's been a complication. Your blood work came back—you're pregnant."

Zoe stared at the doctor, barely aware of Cal's grip tightening on her hand. Had she heard correctly?

Dr. Wright was beaming.

"So we'll have to postpone this operation for at least nine months. Call my office for an appointment. We need to get you started on prenatal vitamins and supplements."

"But I just had cramping," Zoe said.

"You may have had spotting, too. Not uncommon with this condition. We'll do another round of tests, but I'm sure you're pregnant. And since I know you were willing to put up with a lot to have this baby, we want to do everything we can to make sure he or she arrives healthy."

Cal swept her into his arms and lifted her, spinning her around.

"You did it, sweetheart. We're going to have our baby after all. What more could we want?"

"Twins?" Zoe said, hugging him tightly as they rejoiced in the news.

Epilogue

Zoe saw Cal across the crowded living room standing on the perimeter, looking a bit overwhelmed. She went to stand next to him.

"Overwhelmed?" she asked.

"A bit. I'm still trying to remember all the names. When you said you had ten brothers and sisters, I didn't realize how many that would be along with wives, girl friends, boy friends and kids. There must be fifty people here."

"They're all happy for us. I told my folks we didn't need a big reception to celebrate our marriage, so she opted for family only," she said with a grin, surveying the room.

It did look a bit chaotic. Some sat on the furniture, others milled around, little children played tag and used the adults to dash behind. There were conversations and laughter. Zoe smiled. It was happy chaos.

Everyone had come to wish them well. Her brothers and sister who had their own place now lived close enough to visit often. She still had five siblings living at home. She loved seeing them all, especially the children.

Her heart was full. This time next year her own child would join the family gatherings. She could hardly wait.

She glanced at Cal. She thought he'd been surprised by

the warm welcome everyone gave him. She knew her family would include him without question since he made her so happy.

Her mom had prepared a huge spread that filled the dining room table, so people could eat as they wished and go back for more. Her father had brought a case of champagne and there had been a dozen toasts to their happiness.

"Any regrets?" she asked.

He looked at her and shook his head. Leaning over, he gave her a soft kiss.

"I was thinking in another year our boy or girl will be here, getting use to this chaos at an earlier age than I'm having to do."

Zoe giggled. "Hard to believe. By then, you'll know everyone and fit right in."

Just then three year old Tessie came up to Cal and lifted her arms. "Up," she said.

He looked at her and then at Zoe.

"Well, pick her up," she said with a smile.

Cal was surprised how light the little girl was. With her dark hair and big blue eyes and rosy cheeks, she was the picture of a beautiful little princess. It made him wonder if his child would be a girl or boy. Either was fine by him.

"You sure it's all right?" he asked. "She doesn't know me."

Tessie snuggled against him and closed her eyes.

"Of course it's all right. You're her Uncle Cal, she's perfectly safe with you and she knows it."

"Uncle Cal," he said with a catch in his voice. "I don't think I ever expected anything like this."

"You're a natural. You'll be a fantastic father. I already

think you're a fantastic husband."

Her heart swelled for this man. He was more than she ever hoped for, and knew she'd love him until forever.

He gazed into her eyes, his love clearly evident.

"I think you're fantastic, too. And every person in your family. Maybe next time we could suggest name tags."

Zoe laughed.

"You'll get to know everybody soon enough. We'll have Thanksgiving, Christmas, New Year's Day coming before long. And then all the birthdays for you to get to know everyone. One thing this family loves to do is celebrate together whenever possible."

"Our child will be surrounded by love," he said slowly.

"Starting with us," she said.

"Starting with us," he agreed.

Did you enjoy this story?
If so, you may enjoy WHEN LOVE SOARS,
Book One in the Viva Espana Series.

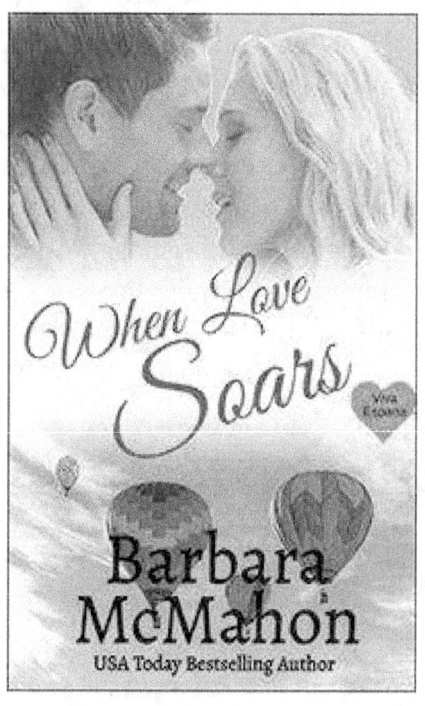

If you liked MIRACLES AND MARRIAGE book,
please consider leaving a review.

For a complete list of Barbara's books, please visit
www.barbaramcmahon.com.